HERE YOU GO

NOL BOOK 3

LEIGH LANDRY

HERE YOU GO by Leigh Landry

Published by Leigh Landry

Lafayette, LA, USA

© 2022 Leigh Landry

This is a work of fiction. Names, characters, places, and incidents either are the products of the author's imagination or are used fictitiously.

1

COURTNEY

COURTNEY COMPLETED THE TRANSACTION ON HER tablet and handed a small paper envelope to the young woman across from her. "Thanks. Enjoy the rest of your weekend!"

The woman smiled and left with her purchase, one of Courtney's favorite shop items: a stern-faced pewter fairy mid-flight, carrying a light purple crystal. People bought Courtney's creations for fan pulls, birthday presents, and children's room decorations. But September meant shoppers were now on the hunt for tree ornaments and holiday gifts, even though it was still ninety degrees in City Park at the monthly Arts Market.

Courtney wasn't about to complain about early holiday shopping or the heat, because it all equaled more sales right when she needed them. This year she'd have to budget for her own gifts and Lucas's new therapist as well.

She looked up to greet the next potential customer approaching from the side of her table. "How are you this—"

Courtney immediately recognized the redhead standing across her table. It had been a long time since she'd seen this old friend in person, but no one could forget Josephine Broussard. Even if she wasn't front and center on every festival stage or on every channel for national interviews, you didn't forget her warm, welcoming confidence.

"Jo! Oh my gosh. It's so good to see you."

Courtney scooted around the table to hold out her arms. Jo met her with a huge smile and an even bigger hug.

"You, too." Jo released her embrace and held Courtney at arm's length to examine her. "You look *amazing*."

Courtney glanced down at her white T-shirt and light wash jeans. A far cry from the edgier clothes she used to rock on stage. Her hair was a lot longer too—a messy, shoulder-length blonde bob she could leave unattended for more time than the pixie cut she'd had when she last saw Jo.

The "amazing" bit was obviously a lie. Or at least an exaggeration. But Courtney wasn't about to correct her on it.

"Thanks," she said. "You look fabulous, as always."

Jo was also in jeans and a T-shirt, but her darker jeans and deep green tee looked more put-together than Courtney's standard market day uniform.

Jo touched her cheeks. "I swear, I think there's still makeup caked on from last week's TV thing."

"I saw that one!" Courtney had watched the televised interview in which Jo and the rest of her country band discussed their success, Jo coming out, and the positive reaction from their fans. "I'm so stinking happy for you! And the band. It's been so awesome to watch everyone learn what a star you are."

Courtney had known the singer long before they were both regulars in the New Orleans music scene. They'd both taken voice lessons at the same place when they were teens. Despite most of the other vocalists having competitive relationships, Courtney and Jo had formed a respectful, supportive friendship. They bumped into each other around the city at festivals and events and each other's shows, but Courtney hadn't seen much of her since Jo's band skyrocketed five years ago.

"Stop." Jo waved a hand in the air but couldn't hide her grin. Then she gestured at the items on the table and the ones hanging from display stands. "Look at *you*! This stuff is unbelievable." She picked up a winged cat and held it up to the light. The morning sun sparkled in the green crystal that matched Jo's irises. "I'd heard you were doing well with this, but I can't get over how beautiful these are."

"Thanks. I'm glad people seem to like them as much as I do."

After her own band broke up, Courtney had picked up jobs when she needed to pay her bills. She filled in the gaps during slow seasons by waiting tables or serving drinks at touristy places in need of part-time help, but her heart was in her craft. She couldn't imagine doing anything else.

Anything else except singing. But that chapter of her life was finished.

"Looking for something specific this morning? You can't possibly have come to the market just to see me and my fairies."

Jo put the winged cat back. "Actually, I did come here for you."

"What can I help you with? A gift for someone?" Courtney remembered when Jo came out publicly and introduced her girlfriend, but Courtney didn't keep up with the news and was hesitant to bring it up or assume they were still together.

"I'm hoping I can help you," Jo said. "You and the rest of the band."

The rest of the band.

There hadn't been a rest of the band—or any band at all—for three years.

"We aren't playing." She stumbled over the words like she did every time she had to explain the situation.

"I know, I know."

Jo's stammering couldn't hide the excitement reaching all the way up into her eyes. Courtney regretted that she'd have to squash that excitement in a moment.

"But if you're interested in playing again," Jo continued, "even just as a onetime thing, I might have the perfect event."

They'd been presented with "the perfect event" enough times over the last few years that Courtney knew better than to trust it. The words were code for: definitely not a thing we want to do. Most of the offers were for gigs they would never take, even when they were playing regularly. None were worth the logistical headache of coming out of retirement.

Jo held up both hands. "Before you say no, let me tell you what it is. Then you can decide if it's worth bringing to the rest of Danger Dames."

Courtney flinched at the "rest of" part of the sentence. But she couldn't tell her old friend no. Not without hearing her first. "What's the event?"

"A music festival. We're going to showcase female and nonbinary musicians, and it'll benefit a couple local organizations that support queer youth. We're calling it Artemis Live."

Artemis. Goddess of many things, but notably regarding this, a fierce protector of young children. And while there's debate over the specific nature of her sexuality, the goddess clearly has no tolerance for patri-archal bullshit. A perfect patron for Jo's choice of charities and the type of event Courtney would love to be part of.

She absorbed the information and considered the feasibility. The idea would be dead in the water if it was some small fundraiser. While the band normally couldn't all agree on a cause to support, this was big enough to appeal to half the egos and a cause they could all get behind.

But the whole getting the band back together thing?

While that chapter of her life was over, Courtney couldn't deny that she missed it. Not the bickering or management nightmares. She missed singing. She missed the synergy of the group when they were nailing a tune. And she missed performing, too. The energy of a crowd fed her in a way nothing else did.

She loved what she did now, but it was a different type of creative fulfillment. The performance aspect was missing. And she didn't realize how much she still ached for it until Jo showed up, dangling this carrot in front of her face.

But even if she could get the remaining band members on board, there was still one major hurdle.

"It sounds great," she said. "But..."

Jo frowned as the excitement faded from her eyes. She knew exactly what Courtney was hesitant about. "I get it. I do."

Courtney sighed. "When is it?"

"Mid November."

Two months away.

"Jo—"

"I know, I know. It's soon. I don't know how Bryn is pulling this together, but she's getting it done somehow! And I get that you haven't played in a while, but you're an amazing band. I know you can pull it off. It'll be just like old times."

Just like old times.

But which old times?

Courtney had put in a lot of work to mentally block out those last few gigs. It was never the same after...

Well, after.

"It's a fundraising festival, but we're still paying everyone." Jo grabbed Courtney's hand and squeezed. "Just promise me you'll run it by the others."

There was that sparkle of hope again. Courtney was such a sucker for it. The entire country was a sucker for it, which made Jo such an amazing lead singer.

But even if Jo wasn't so convincing, a gig could relieve a little financial stress. At least pay for a couple of therapy sessions for Lucas.

"I'm going to regret this," Courtney said with a sigh. "But I'll talk to them."

Jo squealed softly. "You won't regret a thing, promise. I'll send you all the details later this afternoon. I'll just need to know for sure by the 19th."

A week. To convince herself and get everyone on the same page for once. Impossible.

But something in her wanted this more than she'd wanted anything for a long time. More than she was ready to let herself admit.

She held up a finger to wait, then wrapped the cat fairy Jo had been eying earlier in tissue paper and tucked it into a bag. "A thank you for inviting us to play."

"Oh, no. I couldn't," Jo said. "Let me pay you for it."

"I insist." Courtney gave her an inquisitive grin. "Maybe it's a gift for someone?"

Jo's own smile reappeared, stretching wide across her face. "I was thinking Molly would love it."

"Then you have to give it to her. My treat. As a thank you for inviting us to the lineup."

The women hugged goodbye, restating how good it was to see each other and how they hoped to meet again soon.

How soon was the question.

Once Jo disappeared into the crowd, Courtney pulled out her phone and found the group text thread far down in her messages. Longing crackled through her at the sight of those names. Longing for those faded friendships. For the laughter and playful bickering, the hugs and tears...

Despite the way things had ended and despite her lingering anger and sadness, Courtney missed it all.

She missed *them*.

Her fingers hovered over the screen while she second and triple guessed what to say and whether to say anything at all. But she'd promised Jo, so she sent the text.

Hey. Can we meet tomorrow? I have... something...

2

VANESSA

A QUICK SCROLL THROUGH THE SEARCH RESULTS confirmed that no employers in New Orleans or any surrounding parishes were interested in hiring an out-of-work guitarist with zero higher education credits.

There went Vanessa's hopes for a career change.

Actually, she got what she was hoping for. Because Vanessa didn't really want to do anything that wasn't related to music.

She closed the website and opened a map. What she needed was a job, not a new career. Something to pay her bills while she took pick-up gigs and subbed in for people until she landed some more reliable streams of musical income.

Lucky for her, this city always needed daytime service workers *and* musicians. She just had to choose a few places to drop off her resume next week. It had been a few years since she made coffee or cocktails or waited tables, but muscle memory and financial desperation would fill in the blanks.

Her phone rang beside her on the couch, and Vanessa froze when she saw the caller on the screen.

"Funeral or wedding?"

Without missing a beat, the familiar rough-edged voice said, "Neither."

"I expected it had to be one of those if I was hearing from you again."

Her cousin Nicole had been a steady presence in Vanessa's life. They were only a year apart and grew up running through fields and coulees together behind Nicole's house at every family gathering.

The last three years, however, had been radio silence between them.

"Still dramatic as fuck, I see." Nicole paused for a second. "I hear you have some extra time on your hands."

Of course, Nicole had heard the news. Musicians talked. And Vanessa's recent exit from Kings of Canal hadn't been a quiet one.

"Looks like. Calling to rub my nose in it?"

As much as she didn't love it, she deserved a good mocking. Vanessa still stood by her decision to leave the band to tour with Kings of Canal. It had been the best strategic move on the table. It was her *shot*. Of course, she took it.

But she'd left Nicole and the others in a lurch.

She'd left her *friends* in a lurch.

So she expected grudges. Hell, she'd hold a grudge if the situation had been reversed.

"Not at all," Nicole said. "I'm not holding on to that shit. You did what you had to do. We've all moved on."

Had they?

She doubted Nicole meant *all* of them. But even more troubling was the knot in Vanessa's gut. The knot that suspected they really had moved on and had forgotten all about her.

Vanessa hated how insignificant that made her feel. Hated even more that she cared. That implied she was the one who hadn't moved on.

But that was the actual truth, wasn't it?

For all her confidence that she'd made the right decision, she ended up here anyway. With no band. No fame or success. Nothing. At a fucking crossroads, looking for a new life.

"So if not to rub salt in my failure, what's this call for?"

Nicole laughed. "I'm not the one who runs around salting the earth behind me."

"Ouch," she said. "But I deserve that."

"I'm calling to see if you want a gig."

"With who?"

"With us, dipshit."

Vanessa struggled to wrap her brain around the offer. "Wait... with Danger Dames?"

"We've got a gig. Maybe. It's a fundraising thing,

but bands get paid. Benefitting some queer youth organizations. I don't know which ones yet." Nicole gave another uncharacteristic pause. "Wouldn't be right without you."

A direct target to Vanessa's ego.

"When is it?"

"November."

Vanessa laughed. "Can't get a sit-in ready to go in two months?"

"I told you, you belong there," Nicole said. "I'm asking you first. I want to know if you're even interested before…"

The trail-off confirmed what Vanessa suspected. "Right. You didn't get *everyone* on board with this yet."

"I'm not kicking that beehive unless I know there's honey in it."

Vanessa knew exactly what that honey was: Courtney's forgiveness.

Nicole might have let the past go, but there was no way Courtney had done the same. Once you crossed that woman, there was no coming back.

Vanessa put her laptop on the couch and stood. She needed to pace. Pacing was always the solution. Or at least the path to one.

"I don't know what you want me to do," she said. "I can't make her okay with what I did."

"Shit no. No one can." Nicole let out an audible sigh. "Just tell me if you're interested."

Vanessa thought for a moment. Of course, she was

interested. She was always interested in playing. With anyone. Any time. Any place.

But did she want to get excited about something that wouldn't happen? Or should she say no and find a more likely path for her life? One that didn't have a very angry speed bump.

Then again, it was kind of serendipity that she was considering her options right when this call came in. Who was she to ignore fate?

"I'm interested, but—"

"Let me handle Courtney. You just show up at Wild Fern tomorrow. Two o'clock."

Nicole "handling" Courtney held little promise. Nicole had the subtlety of a jackhammer. That's why Vanessa had always been the one to break bad news or sit with Courtney while she processed things. Not that Vanessa had been the fuzziest of the group in the feelings department. She was direct but less abrasive than Nicole, and she'd been able to weather Courtney's storms whenever a glitch in their plans forced her to pivot or adapt in a way she wasn't prepared for.

But Vanessa couldn't be the one to break this news to Courtney.

"You're going to tell her *before* we meet, right?"

After a brief pause, Nicole said, "Sure."

There was something in the word that Vanessa didn't like, but she ignored it.

"Okay, I'll see you then."

"I'm sticking my neck out here," Nicole said. "Don't flake."

"I won't."

The call ended with the implied *this time* unspoken between them.

Vanessa stopped pacing and plopped back on the couch in a huff. What the hell was she doing? This was a bad idea. The worst idea.

She grabbed her laptop again and refocused her attention on the map.

No point obsessing about tomorrow. The decision was made. She would be there. Whatever the rest of them did with her return was out of her control.

The only thing in her control right now was deciding which of these places she wanted to work at. She wasn't planning the rest of her life. Just the next few months. Or more. If she didn't find a more permanent spot in another band, she'd clear that hurdle when she reached it.

Either way, this thing with Nicole and the band was just one gig. Nothing to stress about or get excited about. It wasn't her ticket to her dreams.

A fool's dream.

That's what her mother had always called her musical ambitions.

Vanessa still intended to prove her wrong one day. Just not today. And certainly not tomorrow.

She'd be lucky if tomorrow led to anything at all.

3
_____

COURTNEY

"So, what do you think?"

A bird sang his approval from the tree in the corner of the Wild Fern Eatery's courtyard dining area. The Bywater restaurant had always been a favorite meeting place for the band, and the weather was cooperating for their reunion that early September Sunday afternoon. Not too hot. A slight breeze. Big puffy clouds.

When they'd arrived, there had been lots of hugs and excited chatter. Everyone catching up on what had been going on with their lives the past couple of years since the women had fallen out of touch. Courtney had expected things to be awkward, but they'd picked right back up with a comfortable ease, as if they'd spent days apart instead of years.

While they absorbed the details of the gig Courtney had just described, their server dropped off a plate of spinach and artichoke dip with chips and veggies for them to snack on with their drinks. Emily, their pale-skinned, freckled rhythm guitarist with her hair in the most adorable pigtail braids that day, dove into the dip with the biggest chip she could find. Liberty, their bass player who'd legally changed her name just before the band broke up and was now sporting a short curly faux hawk, reached her long, dark brown arm across the table and grabbed a baby carrot to crunch on while she pondered the decision with her characteristic seriousness. Nicole, their no-nonsense drummer, sipped her gin and tonic in silence, eying Courtney through her thick, black bangs.

It was Nicole who cracked a crooked smile first. "Hell, yeah."

One by one, the band members expressed their enthusiastic agreement. They'd all missed playing. More to the point, they'd missed playing *together*.

To her surprise, Courtney felt an overwhelming sense of relief. She wanted this more than she'd realized. More than she was admitting to herself. Especially after Jo had sent her more details yesterday afternoon. Seeing the date written out in the text, along with the names of some of the other bands already lined up and the organizations they'd be supporting, made it all seem real. And, somehow, possible.

"Awesome," she said. "Then I guess the next questions are when can we rehearse, and does anyone know a guitar player we can call?"

Emily and Libby exchanged a concerned look.

"Fine, I'll be more specific. Anyone know *another* guitarist we can call?"

Emily shook her head, then Courtney caught Libby staring at the garden entrance. Out of the corner of her eye, Courtney saw Nicole's lip twitch.

Fuck.

She stared down the traitor formerly known as Nicole, as her other two bandmates squirmed in their seats. But Courtney refused to turn around.

"What did you do?"

Nicole didn't blink and held firm, returning her stare. "What needed to be done."

Courtney closed her eyes and took a deep breath, wondering if she could stay that way forever. If she could just keep her eyes closed and pretend like she didn't know who was now standing behind her.

"Hey, everyone."

Vanessa's voice was smooth and sweet with a dark, husky edge to it, like good bourbon. But unlike bourbon, Courtney didn't want any part of the woman attached to that voice.

Not anymore.

The voice stirred all kinds of memories, though. And not all terrible.

She closed her eyes and fought back the pleasant ones. The ones that made her want to sit and hear everyone out. Memories of lying on the hood of Vanessa's car to stargaze between sets of that long gig in the middle of nowhere. Of cooing at the monkeys grooming each other while the band waited to play for that zoo fundraiser. Of Vanessa's hand on her arm when Courtney realized she was all Lucas had left and what that meant.

But those memories didn't erase the painful ones.

She opened her eyes to find Libby waving awkwardly with her long fingers, while Emily flashed a grimace at their new arrival.

Courtney pushed her chair back and stood, keeping her murderous gaze on Nicole. Then, without looking at the woman behind her, she turned and walked inside.

"Shit," Nicole muttered behind her.

A few steps later, she heard Vanessa's voice. "You promised you'd talk to her *before* I got here."

Courtney headed straight for the bar and took a seat. All the stools were empty at this time of day, which was just the way she liked it. Especially now, so she could fume in peace without witnesses.

She ordered a bourbon and Coke and waited for the inevitable.

The wait wasn't long.

By the time the bartender placed her drink in front of her, Nicole took the next stool over. She didn't say a word, didn't order a drink, just sat beside Courtney in silence.

"We could have used someone else." Courtney took a big sip, letting the bourbon and acid burn the back of her throat on the way down. "*Anyone* else."

"No, we couldn't, and you know it."

"So she's the only guitar player in New Orleans now?" Courtney didn't even try to dilute the venom in her tone.

She wasn't just pissed off that Vanessa was here. Courtney was pissed off that Nicole obviously knew how she'd feel about this and did it anyway. It was a betrayal. This band was full of those.

Nicole rubbed her face with both hands. "We already tried that, remember?"

Of course, Courtney remembered what it was like after Vanessa left. No matter how much they rehearsed or how good the new person was, it just didn't work out, and they never quite meshed. Emily had even swapped over from rhythm to lead for a couple of months, but she hated it. Said it didn't feel right.

Yeah, Courtney remembered all of that.

"Then we won't do the gig."

Nicole smacked a hand on the bar. "Damn it, Court. It's been three fucking years."

"I know how long it's been." It came out as a growl. But Nicole had done a not nice thing here, so Courtney wasn't in the mood to be nice in return. She pointed at the back door of the restaurant where everyone was waiting outside. "And she's the reason we haven't performed together in all those years."

With a heavy sigh and a softer tone, Nicole said, "And she's gonna be the reason we get to play again.

All of us. Just like before. You said you want that. Don't even try to deny it. I saw how excited you were."

"That's before I realized you were ready to stick a knife in my back."

Nicole rolled her eyes. "You're just as fucking dramatic as she is. You know that?"

"Do not compare us."

"Why not? Scared?"

"Stop baiting me," Courtney said. "I'm not the one that bailed on all of us. I'd never do that. We're not the same. At all."

"Fine, not like that. But you need to get over this, Court. Otherwise, you'll cost all of this gig, and then how different would you be?"

Her back stiffened at that.

Nicole was right. If she ruined this for everyone by holding on to her grudge, then she would be doing the same damn thing Vanessa did.

She took another long sip of her drink, then took an even longer breath, still processing what she knew she had to do, but definitely didn't want to do.

"How did you know about the gig?" Courtney hadn't told them about it after she spoke to Jo yesterday. Just said she had something she wanted to run by everyone.

Nicole shrugged. "I'd heard about the festival from Bryn. When you said you had something all out of the blue like that, I knew it had to be something big.

Figured that was it. So I rolled the dice and called Vanessa."

"Always the gambler."

"I win most of the time," Nicole said. "And I was right on this."

"Were you?"

"I'm not asking you to forgive her," Nicole said. "Hell, I don't know if I've forgiven her. But I am asking you to do a gig with her. With all of us. Together. One time."

Courtney looked up from the last of the dark liquid in her glass. "It isn't just one time. We'll need to rehearse."

"Jeez. Whatever. Can you just do it?"

"Do what? Forget how she walked out on us? Forget that we haven't played together for three years because of it? What am I supposed to do here?"

Forgive how Vanessa was supposed to be their friend?

Although she couldn't say it out loud, that was the part Courtney couldn't get past. All the laughter, all the shared tears, all the comforting and support... none of it meant anything. It was just a business decision for Vanessa. If it had been someone else, maybe Courtney could understand that. But they'd been friends. Or so she'd thought.

"The gig, Court," Nicole said, her voice low and firm. "I'm asking you to do this one gig. If not for yourself, then for the rest of us."

Damn it.

Unlike Vanessa, Courtney felt responsible to her bandmates. She'd never let herself be the holdout vote for something the rest of the group wanted so badly. And for what? A grudge?

No, it was more than that. It was a betrayal. By someone she'd considered a friend.

But Nicole was right. She needed to let it go. At least for a little while. She could keep up all the walls she wanted, as long as she did what the band needed her to do. Show up and play.

Courtney swirled the ice in her glass and downed the last of the watery bourbon and Coke. Then she set the glass on the bar and stood. "Fine. I'll do it."

4

VANESSA

THAT DAMN BIRD CONTINUED TO SING ABOVE THEIR heads like nothing was wrong. Vanessa loved birds, but this one was drilling a hole in her brain with his incessant mating call.

She already wasn't graced with much patience to begin with. Waiting in this courtyard while one woman decided her fate was more than she was equipped for.

But this wasn't just any woman.

It had killed Vanessa to not even see her face before Courtney walked off. She didn't get a chance to look her in the eyes and apologize.

Had she been planning to apologize?

Maybe. Vanessa had decided to wing it and speak from her heart, but Courtney denied her that opportunity. Vanessa supposed she deserved the cold shoulder.

After all, she'd been the one to turn her back on them first.

Vanessa looked over her shoulder at the restaurant door. "This was a bad idea. I should just leave."

"No." Emily grabbed her arm. Her big, light brown eyes pleaded with Vanessa. "Stay. You deserve to be on this gig as much as any of us. But if you tell Court I said that, I'll murder you and they'll have to make a podcast about it."

Vanessa laughed, grateful for the levity. She'd missed these two more than she'd realized. They'd come into the band all those years ago as a package deal. Best friends since kindergarten. Libby talked tough, but Vanessa knew from the way Emily had staunchly defended Libby during her transition that Emily would follow through on any murder threats. And she listened to and watched enough crime shit to know how to get away with it.

"Court will never agree to me coming back."

Libby shrugged. "We can outvote her."

"Two wrongs just suck double," Emily said. "Besides, she's so stubborn, she'd bail entirely if we pulled that. And finding another singer? While we're already a mess? No, thanks."

"Why does she get to have a stranglehold on everything?" Libby asked. "Why are we all tiptoeing around her mood?"

"Because it's not a mood," Vanessa said. "And I'm

the one that broke this band. Not her. So be mad at *me* if this doesn't work."

"Oh, don't worry. I'm still mad at you," Libby said with a wink.

A wink and hard feelings. Vanessa guessed that was the best she could hope for.

Emily hissed, "She's coming."

Vanessa stood and turned to face Courtney, bracing herself for the long-overdue conversation they needed to have.

What she really wanted to do was leave. This was one gig. It wasn't worth all of this drama.

But the universe had put this opportunity in her path right when she needed it. Playing on stage was like a drug, and Vanessa was in withdrawal. Sure, it was just one show. She still needed something more lasting. But this was what fate had handed to her. Who was she to say no to fate?

Her breath hitched in her chest the moment she saw her former friend face to face again. Years of memories came flooding back, in a way they hadn't when she'd seen the rest of the band. They'd all been close, but she and Courtney had formed a deeper bond. They often hung out apart from the group, chatting and laughing about nothing most of the time. Thousands of tiny moments filled her brain, along with the aching void of the last three years.

"Can we talk?" She gestured at some chairs under a nearby oak tree.

Courtney stopped in her tracks and stared at Vanessa a second before giving a quick nod, her long, wavy blonde bob bouncing with the motion. Her hair was much longer than the last time Vanessa had seen her, but it still suited her.

Vanessa suddenly realized that one little nod was making her stomach do flips.

She was just nervous about this conversation and what it meant.

Right?

They each sat in a plastic white chair angled toward each other. Courtney crossed her legs and tapped her foot in the air. Fuming. Terrifying. But also kind of… cute.

What the hell?

Fuming wasn't cute.

Except that little snarl plastered on Courtney's face *was* pretty cute. Less menacing and more hissy, terrified, half-feral kitten.

"Okay, so, first things first." Vanessa fumbled for the right words. She wasn't the kind of person who rehearsed speeches or prepared for conversations ahead of time. She trusted herself to find the right words at the moment. Today, however, the words weren't coming out as smoothly as she wished. "I'm really sorry about the way things went down."

Courtney's foot stopped air-tapping as her gaze snapped to Vanessa. "No, you aren't."

Great. She was even more pissed off than Vanessa had planned for. Jeez, this woman could hold a grudge.

But she wasn't wrong. Not entirely.

"Fine. I'm not sorry I took an opportunity. It was the best move for me, and I'm not sorry I took my shot."

Courtney grunted. "You're only sorry it was a dead end."

It wasn't exactly a dead end. That band just never took off like she'd hoped. Like she'd been promised. They did well enough, but they didn't see what she'd gambled.

And then there was the other dead end.

But none of that mattered now. Not as far as this conversation was concerned.

"I'm sorry you and the others were hurt by my choice."

"You're sorry *you hurt us*," Courtney corrected. "Fuck that passive shit. You hurt us. Own it."

Courtney would make this sting as much as possible. Fine. Vanessa had earned this penance, or whatever it was.

"Okay, you're right." Vanessa paused to make sure every word sank in. "I'm sorry I hurt you."

Silence.

Complete fucking silence.

Courtney just sat there like she was waiting for more. But more what? Vanessa had just apologized. What else did Courtney want from her?

Vanessa swallowed her pride and said, "I'd really like to do this festival with y'all."

Courtney stared her down, biting the inside of her cheek like she did when she was nervous or angry or pretty much all the time.

Eventually, she stopped biting long enough to say, "Fine."

Vanessa relaxed a little. She hadn't realized how much she'd been counting on Courtney to agree to this. How much she missed playing with these women. Even the pissed-off woman sitting beside her.

Especially the pissed-off woman beside her.

"So you forgive me?"

Courtney let out a biting laugh. "Fuck, no."

Vanessa flinched at that. "What do you mean, no? I thought you said—"

"I said we can do the gig together. That doesn't mean I forgive you. The two aren't mutually exclusive."

"So we're supposed to play this show with open hostility in the air? What the fuck, Court? How is that supposed to work?"

"I don't know," she said. "But it'll have to."

Vanessa struggled for what to say next. She knew she couldn't demand forgiveness, but she also knew what doing a gig was like with bad vibes between band members. It was going to suck.

This wasn't what she'd come back for. What she'd been hoping for. What she *needed*.

But she knew Courtney before today. If she'd decided to stay angry, then that's how it would be.

Vanessa didn't have to stick around for it, though. Not anymore. Not if Courtney didn't want her there.

She stood and looked down at Courtney. "Have Nicole text me when y'all decide to have rehearsal."

As expected, Courtney didn't respond. She just lifted her little nose higher in the air.

If Vanessa had learned one thing this past year, it was to not stay where she wasn't wanted or appreciated. And she couldn't make anyone appreciate her. If Courtney was going to be like this, fine. Vanessa didn't have to stick around for the abuse, though.

She stormed off, pausing only briefly to tell the others she was leaving.

"Wait," Libby said. "Aren't you staying?"

Emily fiddled with the ends of one of her pigtails, confusion etched on her face. "Nicole said Court was on board."

Vanessa exchanged a knowing look with Nicole. "She is. For the gig. I'm not staying and ruining your hang, though. I'll see you all at rehearsal."

Then she spun around, blinking back furious tears and stomping out of the courtyard while they shouted goodbyes to her back.

5

COURTNEY

A WEEK LATER, THE HEAT RETURNED, AND IT FELT like peak summer once again. Courtney wiped the sweat from her brow with the back of her gloved hand, grateful for the tiny patio cover shielding her from the sun's direct rays.

She and Lucas had grown up here, and she'd taken over rent after her mother had bailed on him. Now she was glad to be in this little shotgun house in the Bywater again. The cozy backyard gave her a perfect workshop space. She didn't need much room to do her metal casting projects, but working outdoors helped with ventilation and mess.

Using a small paintbrush, Courtney spread baby powder over the three acorn shapes in her handmade silicone mold and clamped the two pieces together. Next, she scooped the slag off the top of the contents of her melting pot. Then she picked up the pot and aimed the spout, pouring liquid pewter into the mold.

These would be acorn necklaces. A recent addition to her offerings that should make nice gifts. She'd sourced the acorns from sidewalks and parks around the city, all from different types of oak trees. Then she'd used them to make custom molds. Courtney was hoping they'd be a hit with both tourists and holiday shoppers over the next few months.

She'd been doing well, but she wanted to up her profit goals for the rest of the year. They'd soon have nice fall weather for the City Park market days, and she'd signed up for some festivals and Christmas booths. Those extra local events through the holidays, plus her online sales, would hopefully carry her and Lucas until the spring festival season. If she hustled and maybe worked on her advertising game, she could save up for a small 3D printer next year. Then there'd be no limit to the custom designs she could offer.

She glanced at her watch, noting the time to make sure she left the metal cooling long enough, then headed inside to where Lucas sat on the floor. His lanky legs were spread across the living room rug. She tapped his shoe with her own as she passed.

"Put your dishes in the sink. Sage is going to be here any minute."

"Why?" Her brother's fingers worked furiously on the controller, and his eyes never left the TV. "She's seen worse in here."

"Don't be gross," she said. "Just put your plate in the sink, at least. Don't you have to study, anyway?"

"As soon as I clear this level."

As far as she knew, that could take three minutes or three hours.

Courtney began washing what was in the sink, and a few minutes later, the doorbell rang.

"Lucas. Plate. Now."

"Fine. I'm coming, I'm coming."

He paused the game and scrambled to his feet while Courtney opened the door. Sage stood in front of her with a stuffed tote bag over one shoulder, a huge chunk of some pale blue crystal dangling from her neck, and the biggest grin on her face.

"Come in," Courtney said, holding the door open.

"Hey, Sage." Lucas dropped his plate in the sink on top of the other dishes with a loud clank.

"Hi, Lucas." Sage radiated sunshine through the house as she passed through the tiny kitchen. "I hope this wasn't a bad time."

"No, of course not," Courtney said.

Sage had texted on her way home that she wanted to swing by for a second. Courtney had met her a few months before at a local arts festival where their tables were next to each other. Sage made miniatures for role-playing games, and Courtney had been impressed with her work and charmed by her delightful personality. The two had become fast friends and met regularly to discuss their craft and business and life.

"Lucas was just going to study," Courtney said. "Weren't you?"

"Yeah, I guess," he said, turning off the game. "I was about to die, anyway."

He disappeared down the hall, and Sage sat on the couch. Courtney flung Lucas's sweatshirt out of the way.

"Sorry about that."

"Not a problem," Sage said. "How's he been doing?"

The last time they'd talked, Courtney had been looking for a new therapist for him. He'd been in an aimless funk since graduation that spring and nearly missed the enrollment deadline for his first semester of community college. It had taken every ounce of energy she had just to drag him through the high school finish line.

Courtney was exhausted by the end, but she couldn't afford to slack off now. She couldn't let him miss opportunities and mess up his future. The kid had dealt with enough. He just needed someone looking out for him. Courtney had never planned to be that person, but she was the only one left, and it was her responsibility.

Lucas had always been a kind and dependable kid, even with no stability at home, but he needed someone to believe in him while he figured out what he wanted to do with his own life. Courtney was more than happy to fill that role.

"Better," she said. "The new therapist seems to be helping. He's going to classes, and he even got a job."

"Oh yeah? Where?"

"Gary's. He's doing prep work in the kitchen."

Sage thought for a minute. "That touristy little place near Frenchman? Good for him." Sage held up a finger adorned with a copper and rose quartz ring. "Speaking of work, I was wondering if you've ever considered teaching."

"Teaching?" The last thing Courtney wanted to do was stand in front of a room full of Lucases. Or worse, a room full of kindergarteners. "You do not want me in a classroom."

Sage laughed. "Not like with books and tests or any of that. And no college degree required."

Good, because Courtney didn't have one of those. Taking care of Lucas had saved her from deciding whether to continue her education. Since she'd ended up a musician and artisan anyway, the debt wouldn't have been worth it for the "experience" or whatever the hell they were selling it as these days. She was only pushing Lucas into more schooling because while he was undecided on a potential career, he had interests in technology and graphic design, both fields that might benefit from advanced education.

But Courtney wasn't sure she was cut out for any kind of teaching. Or even what kind of opportunity Sage might be talking about that didn't require a degree.

"I rent a room in an art gallery downtown where I hold workshops and classes once a week. It's like my video tutorials, but in person."

That's right. Sage had a YouTube channel. Courtney knew her from the festivals and her online shop, and she sometimes forgot that a large part of Sage's income came from advertising on those videos. She'd tried to talk Courtney into starting a channel of her own, but Courtney didn't have time for that sort of thing. Not now, at least. Maybe once she got Lucas on his feet a little more. Or maybe she could pay him to be her assistant. Her brother was pretty good at computer stuff. Maybe he'd be good at the editing and whatever else she was hopeless with.

"That sounds fun. Especially if it's like what you're already doing in the videos," Courtney said.

"Oh, it's a blast. I love interacting with people. Can't exactly do that on video. I thought I'd hate it, but I keep the sign-ups small, so it's more of a one-on-one interaction experience. Like tutoring more than lecturing a big class."

"Sounds great for you," Courtney said. "Sorry, I don't quite understand what you're asking me here."

"Well, as much fun as the classes are, it's kind of a big commitment for me to come up with stuff every week. So I was thinking about tag-teaming with someone. Or offering some joint projects, maybe. I'm just throwing out ideas right now. Nothing solid. I want to have the right person on board first. So what do you say?"

"I don't know." Courtney really didn't. She'd never considered anything like this. "My setup here isn't portable."

"Oh, I get that." Sage's voice trilled with excitement. "Maybe you could do some resin mold projects instead of metal? Just a thought. We could have a brainstorming session later. I just want to float the larger idea first."

Courtney had worked with resin before, but she preferred metal. Metal was strong and had glitz. But resin was an easier beginner project. And safer. She could see potential to combine her methods and supplies with some of Sage's projects.

"Maybe."

Sage held out her hands. "Okay, let's go with that." She hopped to her feet and grabbed her tote bag. "I'm going to let that idea bake in you and check back to see if you have more thoughts or questions in a few days. We can talk fiddly money bits and details later."

Courtney stood and walked with her to the door in a stunned daze of Sage-hype. "Sounds good."

When they reached the door, Sage clapped her hands excitedly and gave Courtney a big hug. "Eek, I'm so excited." Then she pulled back. "Not to pressure you."

"Don't worry, I've got enough pressure elsewhere. This doesn't stress me out."

Sage raised her brow. "I thought Lucas was doing better?"

"He is," Courtney said. "It's a band thing."

"Oh." The words sank in, then Sage gave an exaggerated, "Ohhhh! Does that mean you're getting back together?" With an excited little gasp, she added, "Will there be new music?"

"No, it's just for one show."

"And that's stressing you out? I thought you said last month that you missed playing. This sounds like a good thing."

"It would be," she said. "If it didn't mean I have to play with Vanessa again."

"Sorry, I don't remember everyone else's names." Her eyes widened. "Did you two have a *thing* or something? Is that what happened?"

Courtney tossed her head back and barked out a laugh. "No. We did not have a *thing*."

A long time ago, they'd been friends.

But *just* friends.

The idea of anything else was ludicrous. Possible, sure, since she was only attracted to women and Vanessa was bisexual. But despite their friendship history, they could no longer exist in the same room together for more than a few minutes. *Dating* each other sounded like a recipe for disaster.

Of course, Courtney hadn't always despised the sight of Vanessa. Hell, she couldn't deny the woman was stunning. She still had those long, dark waves that fell past her shoulders and still rocked the tightest pair of black jeans she could find. Even her makeup choices were the same: thick black eyeliner and very little of anything else. Her tanned skin was still flawless, so she didn't need to cover anything up. Only glam up or goth up if she felt like it.

But the most stunning thing about Vanessa was her talent. She was the most naturally skilled guitarist Courtney had ever played with. Talent was always sexy.

It didn't matter how talented or sexy someone was, however, because Courtney had been forced to make some hard boundaries for herself years ago. She'd watched her mother throw everything away for one abuser after another. The ones who weren't abusers were still flat-out takers. And her mother had been happy to give. That left Courtney to clean up the mess and take care of Lucas. Even if she'd had time to date, Courtney had long ago sworn she'd never fall like that for anyone.

As for Vanessa specifically? Betrayal aside, dating a bandmate was a bad idea.

Dating *Vanessa* would be an even worse idea.

From what Courtney had heard, Vanesa's more recent bandmates had discovered both facts.

"Sorry, didn't mean to jump to conclusions," Sage said.

"It's fine. It just... isn't that." Courtney wasn't sure how to explain everything. Or at least how to explain everything in a brief summary that Sage might understand. "She ditched us for another group. But the rest of the band wants her in for this reunion gig."

"And that's a problem?"

"It's a *big* problem." Courtney tried not to snarl with that, but she was pretty sure she failed at the attempt. "I don't trust her."

Sage looked confused. "Do you need to trust her to play? Sorry, I don't know how this music stuff works."

She wanted to say yes. Of course, she needed to trust the people she played with. But that was a different kind of trust than what they were talking about now.

The performance? *That* she could trust Vanessa with. Always could.

But did she need the other kind of trust to play on stage together?

Nicole had been right. Courtney needed to get over herself and just do this gig.

"I guess not."

Sage smiled brightly. "Then it sounds like you don't need to stress about that either."

Courtney sighed.

Sage was right. Nicole was right. Everyone was right.

She just had to get over this.

Or at least get through it.

6

VANESSA

Vanessa was already three drinks in when she heard the rap on her apartment door.

"I'm coming," she shouted from her kitchen floor.

She wasn't drunk. Three drinks didn't make her drunk. Not anymore. She'd just chosen to sit on the linoleum because it was closer to the gin. Bringing the bottle to the couch had sounded like a bad idea.

See? She wasn't drunk yet. But she intended to be soon enough.

She swung the door open and immediately turned away from the man standing there.

"Well, hello to you too," Garrett said, closing the door behind him.

Vanessa plopped on the couch and pointed across the room. "Box. Take your shit and go."

Garrett stood in place and examined her for a moment. He was in his typical Sunday casual look—

faded jeans with a graphic tee and sneakers. His dirty blond hair was a rumpled mess, no doubt still sticky from the previous night's show and... festivities.

He shifted his gaze from Vanessa to the box, then scanned the rest of the room. "Jeez, Vanessa. This place is even worse than normal."

He wasn't wrong. But he was wrong to think his opinion on the fact mattered.

"Box."

Garrett had texted to say he was a couple of blocks away and wanted to swing by for things he'd left in her apartment. A change of clothes. A pair of sticks. A graphic novel. There were a few other things in the box that weren't hers, but she wasn't sure they were his either. He could toss them or not. She didn't care.

Him picking up that shit saved her the trouble of arranging a meeting some other time. She didn't want to run into him with the rest of the band or whoever he was with some other day.

She'd already had two drinks when the text came in, so she should have told him no. But there wouldn't be a better time for this. Best to just get it over with.

And really, it didn't matter. Seeing him. Talking to him. She was over it all.

Instead of walking to the box, picking it up, and leaving like he was supposed to do, Garrett sat on the couch beside her. "It would be irresponsible of me to leave you like this."

Vanessa cackled at that. "When have you ever

been responsible? About anything?"

But the word prompted the image of someone else who'd said something similar to her once. Someone more responsible than anyone Vanessa had ever met in her life. Someone else with longer blonde hair and hazel eyes instead of Garrett's blue... and way better legs.

Okay, so maybe she was a little drunk.

"I let you walk away," he said. "Which took more willpower than I can normally muster, but it was the right thing to do."

"How noble of you to leash your inner stalker."

"Oh, come on. You know what I mean. I could have pleaded my case. Begged you to stay. Promised I'd change."

"And we'd both know that would be a lie."

"Right. See? I was being responsible."

If that's what his definition of responsibility hinged on, she was even more glad that she got out of that relationship when she did.

"Whatever." She pointed across the room again. "Box. I don't need a babysitter."

"Maybe not. But you look like you could use a friend."

She cackled again, this time letting her head fall against the couch so she could stare at the ceiling.

Yeah, she could probably use a friend. But she'd lost all of those. Lost or pushed away or left behind for something better.

Shit.

She was no better than this clown.

But she wouldn't call him a friend. Not by any stretch of the definition.

"*You*," she said, "were never my friend."

When she pulled her attention from the ceiling back to Garrett, she found that he looked shocked. Vanessa realized that he probably believed what he'd just said. That his definition of friendship, like his definition of responsibility, was so warped that he believed he was a good friend to everyone.

"Do you really think I never cared about you? That I don't still?"

She considered the words. Considered their history. Considered the man delivering the message.

Yeah, he cared. He just always cared about the next shiny thing more.

They'd always had that in common.

"I didn't say you didn't care. I said you were a bad friend."

"I don't see the difference."

"You wouldn't." She pointed once more. "Box."

He looked at the box, then around the apartment again. "Who is he?"

"Who's who?"

"The guy who's got you like this?" He examined her curiously, as if just now remembering who she was. "Or girl?"

"There's no anyone."

"You sure?"

"Yes, I'm sure," she said. "I'd know if I was screwing someone."

"You don't have to be screwing someone to be twisted up over them." He shrugged. "Not me. But you're definitely capable of that."

"Capable of what?"

"This." He gestured at her apartment, then he gestured at her. "And this."

"What was that about you thinking you were a good friend?"

"I'm just pointing out the obvious," he said. "You're a mess, Vanessa. I care enough to point that out."

She scoffed. "Thanks."

"So who is it?"

"I told you, there's no one." She sighed. "It's just band drama."

"There's always band drama," he said. "There isn't always this."

She glanced downward and inspected herself. She was in her oversized Stevie Nicks nightshirt and black leggings with fresh holes in them. From what, she didn't know. This had been her uniform for the past few days. She'd put up a good "not caring" front last Sunday after the band meeting, but as the week went on, she lost the energy for fronts.

Fuck, he was right.

She was a mess.

"I'm too sober for this."

Vanessa walked to the kitchen where she'd left the gin and a half-empty can of seltzer beside her plastic cup. She filled it with ice and made another drink.

"So tell me about it before you do a complete memory wipe. Or at least attempt one." Garett leaned against the fridge. "Or I could help you forget?"

"You wish."

Not even an option. She was now officially drunk, and the offer wasn't tempting.

He grinned. "Hence my offer."

"I thought that was just you being a good friend."

"Can't it be both? Now tell me what happened. Who are you playing with now?"

"No one," she said. "Yet."

"It's not our band drama, so whose is it?"

"Danger Dames. There's a thing they want me to do with them." She laughed and took a big swallow of her drink. "Well, some of them."

"Ah. Someone's still not happy about your exit."

"Something like that."

"But you're in on the gig? Officially?"

"Looks like it."

He tilted his head in confusion. "Then why do you give a shit about what one person thinks about you? Since when is that a thing?"

"I don't."

Or at least, she never did before.

That wasn't true. She cared about what everyone thought of her. She just didn't let that guide her decisions. Most of the time. And she wasn't a person to get blasted because one stubborn woman held a grudge.

Yet, here she was.

She'd stormed out of that restaurant last weekend because she didn't want to spend time anywhere she wasn't wanted. And Courtney clearly hadn't wanted her there.

But the others did. They'd said as much, and she believed them. So why had one person's mood affected her so much? Why did she care about what Courtney did or did not feel about her now?

Fuck.

No. That couldn't be right.

"There it is," Garrett said with a smug grin.

"What?"

"The realization. Your light bulb moment. Whatever you want to call it, it means you've realized you care—and deeply, from the looks of it—about someone other than yourself."

No. She didn't have feelings for Courtney.

Well, friendship feelings, sure. She'd never lost those, even if Courtney didn't feel the same way anymore. But were there... other feelings also?

She'd never considered that before. She knew she had a hot friend. But in this mixture of friendship and hotness, was there also a thread of romantic attraction too?

That couldn't be what all of this was about... could it? Why she was so intent on earning Courtney's forgiveness. Why she'd been so pissed off about how angry Courtney still was. Why she'd spiraled when Nicole called with the rehearsal time and reiterated that Vanessa shouldn't expect anything to have changed.

"I care about other people," she said. "That's not a light bulb thing."

Garrett laughed. "Sure. As much as I do."

She was going to do a murder if he kept comparing himself to her like that.

"I cared about you, didn't I?"

Garrett cocked an eyebrow. "Did you?"

She had cared about him. She wouldn't have put up with him if she hadn't. Right?

If she was being honest with herself, she'd cared most about being the center of his attention. She knew who he was and what they were to each other. But once she wasn't his shiny new object anymore, she'd stormed off in an even bigger display than how she'd left that restaurant.

Vanessa put her face in her hands and rubbed furiously. "I don't know anymore."

"Want me to help you remember?"

She removed her hands from her face and found that smug grin still aimed at her. Reminding her how unused to the word, "No," he was.

For the last time, she pointed into the living area near the front door. "Box. Go."

7

COURTNEY

THE LONG DRIVEWAY HAD ONLY ONE EXTRA CAR outside the two-door garage when Courtney pulled in. Her own car had practically aimed itself at the enormous house in Metairie, remembering every turn of the path to their standard Thursday evening rehearsal space.

Emily's parents had offered their massive backyard workshop for them to rehearse in when the band first came together. Her dad kept the place immaculate, and it was big enough that they had lots of floor space for their gear once they moved the center work table to one side. And there was also a secure shed where Emily housed most of their sound equipment between gigs, so it was available for rehearsing too.

Courtney stifled a yawn as she walked down the path across the back lawn. They had way too much music to run through for her to be tired already.

She hadn't slept well last night, but that wasn't different from most nights. She hadn't slept well in years. If she could fall asleep at a reasonable hour, then she'd wake up panicked in the middle of the night and couldn't fall back asleep. It had started long before she'd been a gigging musician working random late nights, and the added responsibility of caring for Lucas didn't help.

There was a constant fear that she'd screw something up for him along the way. Something she couldn't fix. She had guilt insomnia for things that hadn't even happened yet.

Lucas was helping with some bills now that he had a job. Mostly his own expenses, but every bit helped. She thought easing at least some of the financial pressure would help, but it hadn't. She found other things to worry about. Not paying a bill. Screwing up the paperwork for his school loans. Forgetting to pick him up from a late shift.

So not sleeping wasn't new, but she'd lost her chops for rehearsing on no sleep.

She knocked on the workshop door and was greeted by Emily's adorable space buns and a massive hug. Libby stood behind Emily and waved in greeting, obviously less enthused about Courtney's arrival.

"Nicole will be here in a few minutes," Emily said. "She just texted that she had to stop somewhere on the way."

Good.

Now, Courtney could touch base with Emily and Libby first, then Nicole. Assuming she also arrived before Vanessa, who would probably show up late as usual.

Courtney knew the rest of the band wasn't happy with her. They'd made it clear they wanted Vanessa to stay that afternoon at the restaurant almost two weeks ago. But Courtney hadn't forced Vanessa to leave. She hadn't made her storm off like a spoiled child.

Still, she could tell they blamed her for it.

While Vanessa might have been wrong about everything else, she'd been right about not wanting to play this gig with a ton of resentment in the air. Courtney couldn't help the animosity between her and Vanessa. That wound was too deep and the scar too thick. But she could at least clear the air with the rest of the group.

She gathered up her perkiest tone, trying to channel a little of Sage's sunshine, and said, "So, how's everyone been since our meeting?"

"Fine," Libby grumbled.

Emily glanced at Libby and gave a hesitant, "Okay, I guess."

Courtney looked back and forth between them. "What's wrong?"

"Nothing." Libby turned her back to Courtney and started fooling with her amp.

"You're a terrible liar," Courtney said. Then she turned to Emily. "What am I missing?"

"Nothing," Emily said, then bit her lip. "We're just... not sure how you're going to be."

"What does that mean?"

"You know, if you're gonna be all pissy with Vanessa and make this a whole thing again."

A whole thing.

Great. They were still upset with her about that meeting.

She'd earned their hesitance, she supposed. But she wasn't the one who'd started this. Why were they more upset with her than Vanessa?

"I'm not making anything a thing. Y'all wanted to do this gig, so let's do it."

Libby turned to give a doubting glare. "Really? You expect us to believe you're suddenly gonna be all cool and shit?"

"Not cool, but I can be civil," Courtney said. "I just don't understand why everyone else is cool with her like she didn't fuck us over with no remorse. Like none of us mattered. And why you're all mad at me for pointing that out. Why you're all taking *her* side."

"There aren't sides, Court," Libby said. "There's only the band's side."

"There's no band," she argued. "Not really. This is just one gig."

Emily grimaced and raised her shoulders. "Maybe?"

"What do you mean, 'Maybe?'"

"I might have mentioned to someone that we were

playing together for this, and they might want to book us for a regular thing."

Courtney's eyes widened. It was excitement and terror and more anxiety all wrapped up together.

She'd only agreed to this because it was a onetime thing. More gigs would mean more playing time. More creative food. More money for actual food.

The teaching thing Sage had proposed would be a nice bonus, but it wasn't a lot of cash. Getting some extra money would take more pressure off the holidays. She could worry a little less about bills for a couple months, and they could feel more secure until the next festival season. She could even help Lucas get a down-payment on a used car.

But more gigs also meant more playing with Vanessa. More swallowing her pride for the sake of the group and her bank account. More memories of their friendship resurfacing.

More hope for their future.

"Nicole's here," Libby said, her tone flat. "We can all discuss it together."

Courtney waited in stunned silence on one end of the workshop while Emily answered the door.

She'd come here early to win everyone over... to make sure they were still on her side. But now she was glad she'd given herself extra time to process this news and what it could mean.

Did she even want this?

Her gut shouted out a resounding, *yes*!

But she wasn't one to make impulsive decisions. Emotional? Yes. But she always thought them through.

Maybe she didn't have to worry about this, though. It wasn't just her decision, after all. Maybe the others would be too busy or not want the hassle or commitment. Maybe someone else would make this decision for her.

8

VANESSA

THREE CARS WERE ALREADY PARKED IN THE
driveway when Vanessa pulled in. Looked like she was
the last to arrive.

On one hand, she wouldn't have to endure any
awkward small talk or discussions about their previous
meeting. She could walk in, set up, and start playing.

On the other hand, she wasn't making a case for
having changed. At least she wasn't late. She glanced
down at her phone to confirm that and muttered, *shit*.
Only by a minute, but that wouldn't mean anything.

She hauled her guitar and amp to the workshop in
Emily's parents' backyard. The place brought back all
kinds of warm, fuzzy memories of their rehearsals
together. She didn't have much in her life that gave her
warm fuzzies. She was grateful for their history, even if
they'd never forgive her for hers.

All that mattered now was this rehearsal and this next gig.

Vanessa would just have to stuff everything else down into a deep unnecessary-emotions hole.

They all needed to come together to get through this with as little angst as possible. She wanted this comeback performance to be the best. Okay, maybe not Freddie Mercury Live Aid caliber best, but she could shoot for that. If they nailed half of that magic, they'd be in great shape. Shoot for the stars or you'll never get off the ground. Right?

"Looks like the gang's all here now." Nicole gave a warning smile as Vanessa walked into the workshop and found everyone ready to go, even Nicole's drum set.

"Sorry I'm late."

"You're fine," Libby said.

"But if you were late, it would feel like old times anyway, so no worries," Emily said with a cheerful smile.

Okay, so those were the easy greetings. She knew they would be. No conflict there.

Now to decide whether to extend a greeting to Courtney or carry on and accept that breathing the same air was the best they would do for today.

She wished like hell they could return to the way things used to be. To slip back into their friendship like a pair of well-loved, worn-in jeans. Was that too much to hope for?

"Can we get started?" Courtney pushed away from the wall she'd been leaning against and walked to her spot, front and center.

Carry on with no greeting.

The dismissal stung, and her heart ached for their lost friendship, but Courtney had made her decision. And at least Vanessa didn't have to be the one deciding how to handle this. She hated actively having to think through shit. She just wanted to *do* shit.

"Sounds good to me."

Courtney drank from a water bottle and avoided eye contact while Vanessa set her gear down in her own spot.

"I guess we can talk about the other stuff after?" Emily said.

Vanessa felt like she'd missed something very important just before she arrived. "What other stuff?"

Or maybe something she wasn't in the inner circle to know. Something they were waiting to talk about until after she left.

The thought of that hurt. A lot.

"Yeah," Nicole said. "Let's see how this goes first."

———

TWO HOURS LATER, they'd run through a bunch of tunes and Courtney's husky alto had worn down after so long without singing. But those two hours were enough time to confirm that Vanessa was making the right decision here. Playing with this group again was like coming home.

Even with Courtney's disgust stinking up the place and even with Vanessa's tumultuous realization about her shifting feelings for her former friend, being here with these people and falling back into this routine felt warm and soft and comforting.

That, more than anything else ever, terrified her.

What if she never got through to Courtney? Could she be satisfied with how things were now?

And the bigger question… what if she screwed this up again?

"Now, can we discuss the thing?" Emily asked.

Vanessa took that as her cue, so she put her guitar in its bag and zipped it up. "I can get out of your way if you need to talk about something without me here."

Out of the corner of her eye, she caught the flash of a deep frown on Courtney's face. She had no idea what it meant, and her brain wasn't in any shape to interpret it. Although it was trying anyway to come up with all kinds of horrible meanings for that frown.

"No, you're part of the group," Nicole said. "We're all in agreement that we ride together or not at all. So this concerns you too."

Vanessa listened carefully as Emily detailed the potential gig. It would be an every other week thing at a bar they'd played in before. From what Vanessa remembered, it was an okay venue. She didn't know anything about how easy the guy was to work with, considering this would be an ongoing thing and not a one-off. Handling people and payments was Nicole's territory or whoever arranged the gig. All she knew was they paid the proper amount on time.

"It's not a done deal yet," Emily said. "He just wants to know if we're interested at all, since he knows we aren't officially playing together again. Then he'll check on some things before he offers specifics."

Vanessa kept her lips pressed shut. This was yet another thing she didn't want to decide. Surely someone else would have a problem and it would be out of her hands.

"You already know I'm in," Libby said. "And since you brought it up, that's two of us. Nicole?"

Vanessa noted they addressed the easy deciders first. If one of them couldn't do it, then they wouldn't have to even ask Vanessa or Courtney. Drama-free strategy. Vanessa forgot how much she missed that about these women.

"I was holding out to see if we still had it. But rehearsal was good." Nicole couldn't rein in her smile any longer. "Real good. But part of me wants to see how the performance goes. Or if we can even hold this all together until then."

That was fair, but it still felt like a gut punch.

Because what Nicole really meant was she wanted to see if Vanessa would bail on them again.

"I told him I'd give him a tentative yes or no by next week," Emily said.

Nicole sighed. After a glance at both Vanessa and Courtney, she said, "Then I'm a yes."

Obviously, she hadn't wanted to be the deciding vote either.

Great. That meant it came down to two people.

Libby looked at Courtney. "I know you have an opinion."

Courtney always had an opinion. Or she was the one to spot a roadblock a mile away.

Vanessa rarely found that annoying. Sure, she was disappointed now and then, but she never resented Courtney for warning them of potential risks. Other people got annoyed with Courtney's ceaseless risk-assessing, even if they tried to hide it. But Vanessa appreciated the warning. It came from a place of love and wanting the best for the band and everyone in it.

Shit.

Why hadn't she seen this sooner?

She watched Courtney chew on the inside of her mouth and wanted to wash that worry away for her. She was a beautiful bundle of nerves, and Vanessa couldn't stop staring at her.

Shit, shit, shit.

She no longer had any idea what answer she was hoping to come out of that pretty mouth of hers. Hell, she didn't know which way was up anymore. She was drowning in the realization that she had unwelcome thoughts for this woman who had once been one of her closest friends. How had Vanessa not realized this as *attraction* before now?

Because she couldn't.

She couldn't have romantic feelings for Courtney because that would be terrible for the band.

But if there was no band...

No, if there was no band, it meant Courtney's answer would be no. That she hated Vanessa so much she couldn't get past the perceived betrayal to play together, much less *be* together. If that could ever even be an option.

For the first time that evening, Courtney turned to look at Vanessa. In a small, vulnerable voice, she said, "I could use the extra cash."

The statement and the sound of her voice tore at Vanessa's soul. That sentence meant Courtney was now counting on her to say yes. To help her make some extra cash and help out with the brother she cared for.

Wait, did that mean Courtney and Lucas were struggling?

Vanessa couldn't help wondering if that was her fault. She knew Courtney was doing well with her business, better than ever, but had Vanessa's exit from the band and losing that income hurt them?

No, Vanessa couldn't go down that road. She'd made the best decision she could. She was only second-guessing now because it had been a failed experiment.

Maybe all her attempts at success would be failed experiments. Who was she kidding, thinking she could make it big in this business? It was a lightning strike when that happened.

But what did "make it big" mean, anyway? What would be "enough" for Vanessa?

Her mind spun around how good it felt to play with these women again. How much this felt like home. How she wanted more of this.

But would this ever be enough?

Could it?

She looked into Courtney's eyes and wondered if those could be enough. Those eyes and this band. Because the last thing she wanted to do was hurt people again. Especially the person staring at her now, waiting for her answer.

Vanessa realized she was overthinking this. Drowning in her own thoughts.

From somewhere in her brain, a water safety lesson popped up. Her parents had put her in swimming lessons every summer, and one year they'd talked to the kids about beach safety. One lesson was how to survive when you're drowning and can't tell which way is up: surrender.

Vanessa needed to stop struggling. Stop overthinking.

She needed to trust her intuition and let her truth float to the surface.

The truth was she had romantic feelings for Courtney. Always had, probably. She'd just been denying them.

The truth was also that she wanted to play with this band, whether or not they ever made it big.

She could work out what all of that meant later. And if she was in the band, she'd have time and opportunity to earn Courtney's forgiveness. To maybe, one day, tell her how she felt about her.

For now, Vanessa held Courtney's gaze and gave her answer.

"I'm in if you'll have me."

Courtney stared back in silence.

Emily looked around the room for confirmation. "So I can tell him we're interested?"

"Dependent on schedule and pay," Libby chimed in.

Nicole aimed a big smug grin at Vanessa. "Looks like we're back in business."

Vanessa wasn't sure where this would all lead, but she was glad to be on the path anywhere with these women.

All of them.

9

COURTNEY

"I think it's down here."

Sage's long blonde hair bounced as she navigate the art store aisles, dragging Courtney behind her.

It wasn't this store in particular that gave Courtney icky feelings. It was every store. Most of her stuff was special order tools and materials anyway, so she made lists and orders and rarely needed to spend time in physical stores these days. At least it was a Monday morning and not crowded.

Sage, however, gave the impression that she could bring a pillow and some snacks and live in here. Her mossy green linen pants and loosely draped cream blouse already looked comfortable enough to be pajamas.

"Here ya go."

Sage gestured at the shelves in front of her, and Courtney scanned the different resins lining an eye-level shelf. She hadn't worked with this stuff in years and never used these brands, but Sage thought it was a good idea to use the same materials that students in the class could buy locally. Courtney couldn't argue with that logic.

She grabbed some resin and several different pigment colors, then she moved over to the molds. Of course, she had plenty of those at home, but she wanted some specifically for this project. Anything they could use for ornaments, key fobs, or zipper pulls. They had nice options for a general audience. Courtney grabbed a few silicone molds: seahorses, hearts, dinosaurs, and, of course, fairies. Courtney never left a fairy behind.

"I think these will do." She smiled at Sage. "Now for the fun part."

"Ooh, I like fun."

"This is what I need your help for." Courtney wasn't great at this part. Plus, Sage knew the type of people who signed up for her classes and their tastes. "Point me at the glitter."

Sage grinned. "Music to my ears."

A few aisles over, Sage aimed her at a wall of glitter in all shapes and sizes and colors. Courtney's stomach clenched with instantaneous overwhelm.

She stared at the options for a while, then gave up and squeaked out, "Help."

With a giggle, Sage scanned the shelves and grabbed a multi-pack of different color combinations in small plastic containers with shaker lids. "This should give you plenty of options for people."

"How did you do that?"

Sage looked confused. "Do what?"

"Choose so quickly. And not just the first thing you saw. The exact right thing I needed."

"You can't go wrong with glitter," Sage said. "With selecting it, I mean. The application is a whole other issue."

Courtney doubted the truth of that "can't go wrong" part, but Sage knew the intended audience for this, and she had an eye for shiny things.

"I trust you," Courtney said.

Sage frowned. "You should trust yourself more. Your intuition knows what you need."

Courtney laughed as she put the glitter in her basket and carried everything to the front of the store. "My intuition is definitely broken. Or at least we aren't on speaking terms currently."

"I doubt that," Sage said. "Maybe you just can't see where it's leading you yet, but I'll bet it's someplace fantastic."

"My intuition committed to an ongoing gig with the band."

And Vanessa.

Courtney didn't know how she was supposed to get through the next few weeks. Seeing Vanessa tore open old wounds and left her feeling like she was dooming herself and the band to a repeat performance.

Keeping her anger and hurt in check for one gig would have been hard enough. Setting aside her resentment week after week? Her stomach was already in knots after that one rehearsal, and sleep was even more out of grasp than normal. How was she supposed to keep this up?

But she'd given the band her word. If the scheduling and pay worked out, the first of these bar gigs was in less than two weeks. No turning back now.

Thanks, intuition.

"That sounds like a great opportunity!" Sage, the eternal optimist, didn't see the same speed bumps Courtney did up ahead. How could she? It wasn't her history or her betrayal by someone she'd considered a friend. "Wait, is this about the person you're still angry at?"

Courtney took her place in line and waited for a cashier to open up. "Yup. She's back with us for good, I guess."

"Sounds to me like an opportunity to mend things? Put the past behind you all? Start something new and exciting!"

Courtney turned to Sage and wished she had that kind of sparkle to shine on her future. "I'm doing this for the money. That's all."

"But hear me out," Sage said. "What if the universe has other plans? What if she put this woman back in your path for a reason?"

"To annoy me?"

Courtney regretted the words the moment they left her lips. Something about them didn't ring true.

If she was being honest, she was more annoyed with herself than with Vanessa. Annoyed that deep down she wanted this all to work out. And wanting led to disappointment.

"If that's your lesson, then maybe." Sage laughed. "I'm kidding. I mean, what if this is your opportunity to release your past and this animosity that's draining you, and to find some new light?"

New light.

Damn. She really wished she had half of Sage's sparkle juice. Or whatever Sage ran on.

"My bills are draining me right now," Courtney said, advancing a spot in line. "If these gigs help with that, then so be it. I'll suck it up and deal with Vanessa being in the group if I have to."

Sage raised her brow. "Any particular reason you're holding on to such strong emotions regarding this woman?"

"Who? Vanessa?" Courtney laughed. "No. Absolutely not."

It was a reflex. Her words were a venom-laced sword she'd honed over the last few years. Better to use her anger as a weapon than get cut herself.

But she held more than anger toward Vanessa. Or, at least, she once did. They'd been friends, after all. Courtney's closest friend at the time. Which was why it had hurt so much when Vanessa announced she'd already signed on with the other group and was leaving.

Sage said, "I'm just asking because sometimes powerful feelings can mask... *other* feelings. Ones we aren't ready to deal with yet."

Feelings for Vanessa?

No. Not like that. No way.

She remembered a moment during rehearsal where she'd turned to Vanessa while she was in the middle of a solo. Old performance habit. Vanessa had been lost in the music, eyes closed, long dark hair framing her face while her fingers ran up and down the neck of that guitar and danced over the strings. Courtney had forgotten how much she loved watching Vanessa play. How much she loved standing so close to her on stage.

But that didn't mean anything.

Did it?

"It doesn't matter what feelings I might or might not have for anyone," she said. "I've got to keep my focus on taking care of Lucas."

"But if he's doing better... I mean, at some point, he has to take over and care for himself. Right?"

Yes, that was the plan. And the new therapist seemed to help with some of that. But she couldn't just shove him out of the nest like a baby bird. That boy didn't have a hint of real feathers yet.

"He just needs me to be stable right now. Plus, I don't have the time or energy for a relationship with anyone. So even if I did have feelings for someone, and I certainly don't for Vanessa, it wouldn't matter."

"You don't think it's possible to be in a relationship and be a stable person in his life?"

Courtney had watched her mother divide her attention between her relationships and her children. Her boyfriends always wanted at least equal time with her, but equal time after subtracting those night shifts at the hospital meant Lucas and Courtney were on their own most of the time. And equal time became no time as her mother became more codependent in her relationships and more dependent on Courtney to be resilient and handle things in her absence.

Even if she didn't think that would ever happen to her, Courtney couldn't take the risk that she might slide down some relationship hole she couldn't find a way out of. Besides, people showed you who they were. Her mother and Vanessa had already revealed themselves.

"Not for me." Courtney advanced toward the cashier, waving an arm at her. "Not now at least."

Sage said, "That makes me sad."

Courtney placed her items on the counter and surprised herself with her answer. "Me too."

10

VANESSA

There was an empty table near one wall overlooking the sidewalk, so Vanessa claimed that space to fill out an application while she sipped her black coffee. Spiderwebs stretched across the windows, brick walls, and light fixtures hanging from the high ceiling. The place was ready for Halloween almost exactly a month ahead of time. These people were too excited about it to wait until October first to decorate.

Not that she minded. As holidays went, Halloween was one of the better ones. And the coffee shop's decorations were cool and not geared toward kids. A distinct point in this place's favor.

Vanessa stared at the form in front of her. She'd already filled out the easy stuff. Name. Address. Cell number. Education. But the employment history part got tricky. She couldn't remember the accurate dates of any place she'd worked in the past. It had been a few years since she'd done anything but gigging.

But if she had to get a day job again, this place wasn't too bad. The location on Magazine Street was easy enough to find nearby parking. It was a little brighter and more upbeat than she liked, but the coffee shop she'd first thought of transformed into a bar with live music in the evenings. It would be perfect if she didn't have to perform elsewhere during those hours.

So this coffee shop made an acceptable second choice. The walls were lined with signed photos of local music legends, including Allen Toussaint, Irma Thomas, Trombone Shorty, Ellis Marsalis, and Kermit Ruffins. Jazz wasn't really her jam, but she didn't have anything against it. Hopefully, she'd feel the same way after a few weeks of listening to it nonstop.

If she got this job.

"Must be my lucky month," a deep, familiar voice said above her.

It had been a little over a week since Garrett had shown up in her apartment. She'd love to go the rest of the year—maybe even the rest of the decade—without ever hearing that voice again.

Someone had once described New Orleans to her as the biggest small town in existence. It definitely felt like that some days. Especially days when she was trying to fill out a job application without running into one of her exes. This one in particular.

"Can't we just pretend you never saw me here?"

"You know I can never forget your face."

Ugh. What did she ever see in this guy?

Simple answer: presence.

While he was shitty one on one like this and forced out his dollar store charm way too hard, he was an absolute beast behind the drums. Vanessa was a sucker for confidence on stage.

But his performances were always missing something. Took her a while to figure it out, but her favorite musicians had a bit of vulnerability to balance their boldness. Like Courtney. Her voice had this mesmerizing mix of confidence and openness. Garrett had never been vulnerable for a day in his life.

"Then it was good to see you, Garrett." Maybe if she faked nice, he'd get bored and move on. "Have a great day. Bye."

He pulled out a chair and sat across the table from her. "What are you working on there?" He craned his neck and tilted his head to examine the paper. "Is that a job application?"

"It's none of your business, that's what it is."

"Don't tell me you can't find another band." He let out a little mock-laugh. "You know, you could always come back to play with us. We haven't grabbed a permanent replacement yet."

That sounded like the worst idea in the world. An easy no, for once.

"I've got a band."

"You said that was a one-off thing."

"It was, but we might have a regular gig now."

His eyes widened with amusement. "You're going back with them? For good?"

"For now," she said. "And I'm not screwing them over again, so I'm not taking a bunch of other gigs that might conflict with their schedule."

"You're really all in with them?" He shook his head in disbelief. "I thought you left for a reason."

"And that reason didn't pan out."

With a hand to his heart, Garrett said, "Ouch. Direct hit."

He was feigning hurt, but she didn't care if it had hurt him. It was a shitty situation. He knew it when he'd lured her over there. And she'd fallen for his hollow promises. All of them.

"So you're selling yourself short and getting a day job... for what? Loyalty?" He grinned. "Love?"

"Don't you need to place an order or something?"

"You know, if you come back with us, you wouldn't have to make coffee or whatever it is you end up doing."

"I like coffee," she said, defiance building in her tone.

"I get it. It's me you don't like. Message loud and clear." He frowned at her. "But I mean it, Vanessa. You could come back. I know you're done with me, but you don't have to leave the band, too. We can be adults about this."

Vanessa scoffed. Garrett had never behaved like an adult a day in his life. Whatever that meant.

But that wasn't the point.

She didn't want to go back to that band. Kings of Canal were content to be local musicians. No further aspirations. Which was fine. In theory. But they'd promised her more, and when she realized they weren't working toward that, she'd taken her disappointment and left.

The difference with Danger Dames was that she knew what they were and what the women in that band wanted.

Vanessa had to guard herself against disappointment. Dissatisfaction was her superpower. Sure, it made her strive to always be better at whatever she was doing. But it also left people around her struggling to keep up. To measure up. She didn't want to hurt anyone or make them feel unimportant. But she couldn't control how she felt, either.

An excellent reason to avoid relationships.

Vanessa had left a string of romantic dissatisfaction in her wake. She wasn't proud of it, but she grew bored of relationships easily. Most had ended on a friendly note because she knew enough to cut things off early, long before they became too serious. If she felt an inkling of restlessness, she got out.

But even if it were true that she had feelings for Courtney, and she wasn't ready to admit that yet, she would never want to do that to her. Courtney wasn't a woman you had a casual fling with. Especially given their previous friendship. There was too much at stake. Their potential rekindled friendship. The band. Courtney's feelings.

Garrett had been right. Since when did she care so much about what someone else felt?

Shit. This was real, wasn't it?

Didn't matter. The result was the same.

Vanessa was on a relationship hiatus. And Courtney was especially off-limits.

But winning her friendship again was still on the table.

"I'm not going back," she told Garrett. "Ever."

He examined her and nodded at her form. "We'll see. Maybe you'll feel differently after making a few coffees and settling for that other group for a while."

He stood and walked to the counter, leaving her to fume alone over his use of the word *settling*.

Of course, he thought he and that band were better than everyone else. His over-inflated ego could be seen from space.

Still, he knew her.

He knew her in a way that few people did, because like it or not, they were alike. At least in that way. He knew she'd grow restless and dissatisfied with her current situation, eventually. And he was just pouring gasoline on that preexisting fear.

But she couldn't bail on Danger Dames again.

She wouldn't.

Vanessa felt guilty enough for the last time. After hearing how much Courtney needed that gig money, Vanessa couldn't stop thinking about her own hand in that.

She looked down at the application and had a thought. She needed day job money too. At least for now. But what if she could also help Courtney? To make up for bailing on them in the past?

Courtney would never accept anything, of course, but she didn't have to know about it.

This would take some thought.

And a little help.

Vanessa sent a quick text, then went back to filling out her application with all her fingers and toes crossed.

11

COURTNEY

THE LIGHT-COLORED BRICK BUILDING LOOMED ON the corner of Magazine Street. Vanessa peered through the window and spotted a few open tables inside.

Perfect. She could grab a cup of tea, which Sage had assured her was as delicious and invigorating as the coffee here, and sit while she settled her nerves. She was excited about the new adventure she was about to begin, but she needed a moment to calm herself before she stood in front of a room full of strangers to teach them how to make resin key fobs.

Her body vibrated with anxiety. Not because she feared standing in front of people. Because she wanted them to enjoy the class. She was good at her craft, but she hadn't been tested as a teacher yet and didn't want to disappoint her students.

Courtney loved the idea of doing something new. Sure, she incorporated new pieces and tried out new techniques all the time, but this was a different field. She could sing, and she could metal cast, but could she pull off teaching? To a level she could be proud of?

Courtney entered the building, and her shoulders relaxed. Bright, modern jazz filled the air, and there was an energetic hum from chatty patrons, noisy machines, and dishes clanging as orders' names were called out. The place was decked out for Halloween at the end of the month, which added to its appeal.

She stepped up to the counter and grabbed a menu to examine their tea selections. Then she moved aside in case anyone came up behind her ready to order.

"Check out the Hibiscus Meadow. I think you'd like it."

Courtney bristled at the assumption that the barista might know what she wanted. Then, before she could reply, her brain clicked into recognition.

That voice. It couldn't be.

She looked up from the menu to find Vanessa smiling at her from behind the register. Her dark hair was pulled back in a loose, low ponytail, and she was wearing a wide-collared black shirt that hung off one shoulder to reveal a red tank underneath.

"It's got a green tea blend with hibiscus and strawberry," Vanessa said when Courtney continued to stare at her.

Courtney's brain tripped over the fact that Vanessa remembered she liked hibiscus tea. Sure, she'd had one before every gig. And once, when she'd been recovering from a cold and her fuzzy brain forgot to bring one with her, Vanessa had run out after the sound check to grab one a few blocks away before their downbeat.

But remembering a drink order didn't mean anything. Certainly not that Vanessa gave a shit about anyone but herself. If she'd cared, she wouldn't have left the way she did.

"You work here?"

Of course, Vanessa worked here. She was standing beside the counter.

But Courtney was still too flustered to make sense of this, much less maintain her angry facade. They'd sat through another rehearsal together last Thursday, to prepare for this Friday's gig, and that had gone fine. Courtney had kept things civil, but she'd also kept up her wall.

She'd prepared for that rehearsal. Had prepared to see Vanessa that evening. She hadn't prepared for this at all. Not when she was already worried about her class in a little while.

"Second day," Vanessa said with an uncharacteristic perk to her voice.

Most musicians had day jobs. That wasn't odd. The odd thing was Courtney had never known Vanessa to have one. And she'd assumed Vanessa was still sitting in with other groups, even though she'd left the other one. Vanessa had always been lots of bands' first call when they needed a sub.

She realized she was staring at Vanessa. Examining the woman in front of her. Mentally lining her up with the woman she remembered. Her makeup was a subdued version of what she wore on stage. Thick eyeliner and mascara with nude lipstick and maybe some tinted lotion. Grabbing all the attention for her eyes. Not that they needed any help in the attention grabbing department.

"Sorry, I'm just surprised, is all. I kind of assumed your schedule would be too full for a job."

"Day hours only," Vanessa said. "And... not exactly."

Courtney waved a man ahead of her as she continued to process this information. He gave his order, and Vanessa rang him up like she'd been working there for months. Then he moved along to wait at the other end of the counter.

"I can't believe you're not getting calls for gigs," Courtney said. "I figured your cell would be blowing up once people heard you weren't with Kings of Canal anymore."

Vanessa shrugged. "I got some calls this week."

"I don't understand then. Are you burned out or something?"

Courtney shook her head, confused about why she'd asked the question. Vanessa deserved whatever karmic justice she received for abandoning her friends and not once checking to see how they were doing. Courtney had always thought their friendship would have been worth at least that. But she was wrong.

So the question was just Courtney being nosy.

"Sorry, none of my business." Courtney waved the menu, then placed it beside the register. "I think I will try that tea you mentioned. To go, please."

Even if she needed to roll back her nosiness, Courtney had found a sense of calm in this conversation. Quite a shock, considering how hot she'd been at their last meetings.

Sage was right. Courtney had to let the past go. She didn't have to rekindle their friendship or even forgive Vanessa, but she had to stop chugging that poisonous resentment and move on. For her own sake.

Vanessa rang up the tea and hesitated. "I've got a break coming up in a couple of minutes." Her voice was soft. Very un-Vanessa. "Can I pay for this and maybe we can talk for a bit before you head out?"

Courtney's stomach dropped. It was one thing to chat with a cash register between them. It was another thing to engage in a one-on-one talk.

She couldn't ignore the ache in her gut. The wanting she felt to extend this moment.

No, she was still angry at Vanessa.

Furious.

But she missed her friend. Or at least the moments they'd once shared. Missed those warm drinks together as she calmed her nerves before gigs. Missed their quiet conversations between sets. Missed their coffee runs before long rehearsals.

Maybe if she injected some of those rituals into this teaching thing, that might give her some calm and confidence. After all, standing in front of a room full of people to show them how to do something was a sort of performance. Maybe this tiny routine from their old days, sharing a cup of tea before a gig, would help settle her nerves before she walked down to the art gallery.

She glanced at the clock on the wall. "I have to be somewhere in half an hour. It's just down the road, though, so I have a few minutes."

Vanessa beamed with what looked like relief. Like she cared whether Courtney wanted to talk. And not as a self-righteous point of pride. She seemed to be looking forward to a chat.

Courtney's stomach was now tumbling with nerves and some other feeling she couldn't quite name.

"Great," Vanessa said. "Grab a table wherever you want, and I'll find you in a couple of minutes."

12

VANESSA

ONCE HER BOSS TOLD HER TO TAKE TEN, VANESSA hurried around the counter and headed straight for the door. She'd already scanned the inside tables and knew that Courtney must be waiting outside.

Or she left.

Vanessa tried not to dwell on that possibility. Sure enough, she found Courtney sipping her tea at a patio table.

Of course, she was waiting. She'd said she would. Courtney never bailed on anything she said she'd do.

Even with the traffic rolling by, it was quieter here than inside, which Vanessa took as a good sign. Courtney was willing to hear her out, not drown her out.

She put a hand on the empty chair and waited for Courtney to nod her invitation before she sat. "How's the drink?"

"Great," Courtney said. "I'm surprised you remembered I like tea."

"You always had some kind of tea with honey in it before gigs. I was hoping I remembered the hibiscus part right."

"You got it right. I used to hate it, but it works." Courtney looked at her cup and shrugged. She'd removed the black cardigan she'd been wearing and had draped it over the back of the chair, revealing her soft shoulders framing a dressy, black sleeveless blouse. "I've grown to like tea even though I haven't needed it for singing in ages. This is one of the best blends I've had."

"I'm glad." Vanessa rubbed her fingers in her lap. "I've only got a few minutes before I need to go back in."

"That's okay, I'm teaching a resin class down the road in a bit, so I have to leave soon, anyway."

That explained the dressy blouse instead of the vintage T-shirts and jeans Courtney normally preferred.

"I didn't know you were teaching classes."

"Only temporary. For now," she said. "It's a friend's class. I'm just taking over a couple of sessions. This is my first one."

Vanessa smiled at that. "Seems like we're both doing new things this week."

Courtney looked inside the giant window beside her. "Do you like working here so far?"

"Yeah, I do." To her surprise, Vanessa enjoyed interacting with customers. And she liked her coworkers and the energy of the place. She might even grow to like jazz. "The reason I took the job was so I wouldn't take any of those calls."

Courtney looked confused. "Calls to play with other bands? Why wouldn't you want to do that?"

Vanessa looked into Courtney's hazel eyes and held her gaze to make sure the message got through. "Because I'm playing with you all. And I want to keep that commitment this time."

Courtney frowned but didn't address the *this time* part of the statement. Her voice, however, reverted to the tightness that had been present during their last couple of encounters. "No one asked you for band monogamy."

"I know. But I didn't want to rely on a bunch of random gigs for money and risk booking something when you guys need me or double book because I'm juggling too many bands."

Courtney looked unmoved by the explanation. "Since when are you so conscientious?"

Well, that stung more than it should. It was no secret Vanessa didn't dot her *i*'s or cross her *t*'s. That was Courtney's department. But that didn't mean she enjoyed the fact being aimed at her like some major character flaw. It was just the way she did stuff. Fast and finished.

Still, in this case, the result of her rush to action

had lingering consequences. The last thing she'd wanted to do was hurt any of them, especially Courtney, but she hadn't thought through that far when she'd left. She hadn't thought about the collateral damage, only her goal.

She didn't regret the decision, only the way she'd gone about it.

"Since I know I fucked up, and I don't want to hurt y'all again."

Courtney didn't respond. She sat quietly and took another sip of tea. Processing. Or sulking. It was hard to tell the difference with her.

"You don't have to say anything. I understand you'll have to wait and see if you believe me. Or maybe you never will." The thought of that hurt more than Vanessa wanted to admit. Even to herself. She'd grown up with her family not believing in her, or at least not in her ability to pull off being a musician, and whenever someone hinted at not believing in her now, all of those old scars itched. "So, tell me how you're doing. How's Lucas?"

"He's... good."

"Uh-oh. That doesn't sound good." Vanessa did some mental math. "He's finished school, right?"

Courtney nodded. "Graduated this spring. Taking community college classes now."

"Well, that sounds okay."

"It is," Courtney said. "It's just... he's had a rough time, is all."

Vanessa wanted to ask more, but she didn't want to push. Courtney's walls were up again, and if she wanted to share more, she would. If she didn't want to share more, prying would only piss her off.

Vanessa settled on the only suitable response. "I'm sorry."

"Thanks. But, like I said, he's good now."

"I'm glad. And you?"

Vanessa really wanted the answer to that question, but a man walking toward them down the sidewalk grabbed her attention and strangled it.

"Something wrong?" Courtney asked.

But Vanessa couldn't respond. Couldn't speak. They were making progress, and this was the last thing she needed colliding with their conversation.

Garrett continued his approach, that smug grin plastered across his face. He stopped when he reached their table.

Damn it.

"Looks like October might be my lucky month as well." His voice had a lightheartedness to it, but malice slithered beneath the surface. "Good to see you again, Vanessa."

What the fuck was his game here? Was he planning to annoy her until she rejoined his fucking band? Not happening.

"That's called stalking," she said. "I'm on a break. You can harass me or try to get me fired or do whatever you came here for in two minutes."

"I just came for some coffee." He extended a hand to Courtney. "I'm Garrett."

Courtney looked at his hand, then up at his face and said in her direct, no-bullshit tone, "We've met."

When not directed at her, Vanessa found Courtney's *don't fuck with me* attitude hotter than a Southern August sidewalk. Vanessa had forgotten how much she loved this woman's ability to command any awkward situation.

Garrett just grinned and removed his hand. "Courtney, right?"

She nodded, but gave nothing more in return.

Courtney had been emotional and flustered during their initial reunion at the restaurant, but even then, she'd been the one in charge of their conversation. And she'd returned to her calm self at both rehearsals.

This was truly annoyed Courtney. Pissed off Courtney could eviscerate someone with a few well-selected words delivered with unwavering firmness.

"Coffee's inside, Garrett," Vanessa said.

"Right. It was good to see you both again." He lingered, grinning still, then disappeared inside the coffee shop.

"Now I understand why you left the band," Courtney said, sneering at the door. "Although that missing piece of the puzzle doesn't explain why you fell for him in the first place."

"I didn't fall for him." It was the truth. Mostly. Vanessa had fallen for the idea of Garrett. The adrenaline rush of their brief, chaos-fueled relationship. Never the man behind it all. "Not really. But yeah, that was a mistake."

Another mistake. She'd been racking up mistakes for a few years.

No more, though.

Courtney looked back at Vanessa, her gaze softening. "Glad you figured that out. He's always seemed pretty awful."

Vanessa had a fleeting reflex to defend the guy. Courtney was right, of course, but Garrett was just looking out for Garrett. He wasn't malicious. Selfishly manipulative? Maybe. But in this case, Vanessa had known what she'd been walking into. It was time she took some responsibility for her own decisions and stopped blaming people like Garrett for the messes she got herself into.

"I'd better get back inside," she said.

"Good luck with him."

"Oh, I'm going to take my time clocking in until someone else finishes with his order. Good luck with your class."

Courtney gave an appreciative smile. "Thanks. I need all the luck I can get with that."

Her lack of confidence was endearing, as always. Courtney had always cared deeply about the audience whenever they played a show. More than anything, it mattered to her that people enjoyed themselves, and that her performance moved them somehow. That deep caring and the weight of that responsibility translated into intense self-doubt before most gigs. It made sense that she'd feel that same pressure and nervousness before this, too.

"You'll be great," Vanessa said.

They both stood, and Courtney said, "Thanks for the tea recommendation."

"Glad you like it." Vanessa bit her lip, debating whether to say anything else or to just let things end on this positive note. "Thanks for talking with me. Even if you don't want to be friends again—and I understand if you don't—I wanted to clear the air a little."

Vanessa held her breath while she watched Courtney consider her next words, holding Vanessa's fate and their future in that guarded silence.

Finally, Courtney found the words she'd been looking for. "I think it's best for the band if we aren't at each other's throats all the time."

Vanessa ignored the searing pain in her gut. "Right. For the band."

They said goodbye, and Vanessa retreated inside, where she could ignore Garrett and lick her wounded pride.

13

COURTNEY

Cleaning up after her own projects was an acceptable part of Courtney's creative process.

Cleaning up after other people's projects? Way more of a buzzkill than she'd expected.

At least she had Sage to help, and the class had gone well. Exceptionally well. The participants' reactions had far exceeded her expectations. People seemed to enjoy the project, and they understood and could follow her directions with no major issues.

"Where do you want to go to celebrate?" Sage asked as she stacked a bunch of paper plates and other trash from one table and tossed it into a garbage bag. "My treat."

"I can't let you do that," Courtney said. "Besides, I'm sure you have things to do."

"Nope. Brooke is at work for another few hours,

trying to finish up a job before the end of the week, so I'm a free bird for a while."

"A free bird?"

"That was a little more dramatic than I intended." Sage laughed. "I adore being in love. Our domestic routines are comforting."

"Sounds nice."

Some days, Courtney thought she might like to try dating again. But then she'd remember all of her responsibilities and the stress she was already under. She didn't want to further divide her time and add the pressure of a relationship to that mix.

Although, having someone who wasn't her brother waiting for her at home sounded nice. But getting to that level of a relationship was the hard part. The part she didn't have any interest investing in at this point.

"So where are we going?" Sage asked again. "There's a tasty new place a couple of blocks away. Mexican-Cajun fusion something or other. I don't know how these food things work. I just know they have amazing blackened shrimp tacos and happy hour margarita specials."

"That sounds perfect." Courtney unmuted her phone and found a text notification from Nicole. A notification she would need a little time and maybe a stiff drink to process. "I definitely could use a margarita. And maybe a pep talk, too."

Sage rubbed her hands together. "My favorite kind

of talk." She looked around at the remaining mess. "Let's speed clean and get to pep-talking!"

THE SERVER DROPPED two gigantic jalapeño margaritas in front of them, and Sage raised her glass. "A toast to a wonderful first class and many more to come."

Courtney raised her own glass, but hesitated. "I thought this was just a two-class deal?"

Sage shrugged with a knowing grin. "Who knows what the universe might have in store for you. Success begets success!"

"If you say so."

"I do." They clinked salt-rimmed glasses garnished with candied jalapeño slices. "Wait. What else are we toasting? Was that a good news text you got? That seemed like an 'I need a drink to take this leap of faith' kind of look."

Courtney laughed. "How do you do that?"

"What?"

"Read my mind."

"I read *people*," Sage said. "I pay attention, and I get a feeling. So I guess I read people's emotions. But not their minds. Not really."

Weirdly, that made sense to Courtney. She wasn't super into woo stuff, but she liked the idea of universal connectedness and energy flow and all the things Sage liked to talk about. They were comforting most days. Other days, Courtney wanted to stew in her discontent while the universe fucked off for a while.

"So, tell me about this news."

Courtney took a big sip of her margarita. It had just the right amount of kick to balance the sweetness. She definitely needed a drink for this upcoming leap of faith. Although this felt more like something she'd already jumped into and was now in the freewheel stage.

"Remember how I told you we might have a regular gig down the road?"

"I think so. You've got that big festival next month, and you said maybe something else, right?"

Courtney nodded and stirred the short straw in her spicy-sweet frozen slush. "Well, it's currently 'down the road.' We start the new gig this Friday."

"As in two nights from now? That's so exciting!" Sage held up her glass again. "To continuing adventures and everything you want within your reach."

"What if this isn't what I want?"

"I thought you were asking the universe for more money a couple of weeks ago? You manifested this!"

"I was asking for more sales, not drumming up old wounds."

Sage shrugged. "Sometimes the universe gives you what you need, not what you think you want. And didn't you say you were excited about playing again?"

Dammit. She had been excited. And she enjoyed playing with them again.

"Yeah, I guess."

"You're overthinking this," Sage said. "I should know. I'm the queen of overthinking, and it never goes well."

"Overthinking feels like my kingdom." Her insomnia had a grip on that monarchy.

"We can co-rule. Or trust the universe more?" Sage motioned with her glass. "To seizing opportunities wherever they lead."

Courtney clinked her glass against Sage's once more, much less confidently this time. Trusting in the unknown wasn't a thing she was comfortable with. The universe, money, *people*... they'd all let her down at one point. Her mother had failed her and Lucas, but she'd taught them two valuable lessons: never count on anyone or anything but yourself, and believe people when they show you who they are.

Sage took a drink while she examined Courtney over the rim of her glass. "What's holding you back from being excited about this? Specifically. Is there a history of bad gigs?"

"No, not at all." That was the one thing she could count on. In the past, at least. They'd never had a truly terrible performance. Even if a gig was in shitty conditions, they always pulled it together and played well.

Well, they'd always pulled it together when

Vanessa was with them. The gigs after she left were another matter.

But with that as part of their history now, with all of that hurt in the air, would they still be able to pull off a good show time after time? Rehearsals were going well, but would that last?

"Then I guess this is about... Veronica?"

"Vanessa." Courtney took another big sip. More of a gulp. She cringed at the cold headache and said, "I ran into her this afternoon before the class."

"You didn't tell me that." Sage shifted in her seat like a little kid settling in for story time. "This sounds good. Go on."

Courtney struggled to describe her meeting with Vanessa. She'd pushed it out of her mind for the duration of the class so she could focus all her attention on her students, but now the scene was running on a loop in her head again. Along with the emotional soup it stirred up.

"It wasn't awful."

"Well, that's a start."

"She's working at the coffee shop down the road."

"Crescent Cafe?"

"Yeah, the one you told me to try," Courtney said. "She's working there to avoid taking a bunch of other gigs to pay her bills. She wants to commit to our band."

Sage leaned back in her chair. "Do you believe her?"

"I believe she *wants* to commit. Whether she'll be able to follow through on that is still to be seen."

"Why would you say that?"

Courtney tried to separate her feelings about not trusting anyone from why she didn't trust Vanessa in particular. This felt justified, and not just as some shitty-but-useful childhood baggage she was lugging around.

"She doesn't have a track record of sticking with things. Bands. People. Anything. She gets restless. I have no reason to believe she won't get restless and leave us hanging again."

Sage gave a sympathetic frown. "Okay, but do you want to believe she's changed? Or at least that she's trying to?"

Courtney's gut agreed with a resounding *yes*, but her brain had other things to say about that.

Maybe it wasn't her gut, but something else. Just thinking about that brief meeting made her pulse kick up again.

"No, my brain doesn't want to believe that," she said.

Sage gave a knowing smile. "But your heart does."

"You're doing that thing again."

"I can't help it!" Sage laughed. "And don't change the subject. The way you talk about her... you're more relaxed. Something's different."

Was something different?

Or was their relationship just sliding back into the way it was before?

Or was this something new surfacing…

"Part of me wants to believe her. Because part of me does want her friendship back," she said. "But I don't know what that means for the future of the band. And I don't want to feel betrayed by her again. It hurt too much."

"It hurt because you care about her."

"She was my friend."

"Was she something else, also?" Sage asked. "Or is she?"

Courtney sighed. "I don't know."

She'd always found Vanessa attractive. Just about everyone did. But Courtney had never let herself think about Vanessa as anything except a friend and a bandmate. A colleague. A work pal.

Who was she kidding?

It had hurt so much when Vanessa bailed on them because she had never been just a work pal.

But was there something else there besides friendship?

Did she want there to be something else?

"It doesn't matter," Courtney added. "That's not a line I would cross with a bandmate, anyway. That would be irresponsible."

Sage raised her brow. "It was irresponsible of me to get involved with my ex of a neighbor, and that turned out well."

"You two were meant to be, though. That's clear to anyone who sees you together."

Meant to be?

Sheesh, Courtney said some weird shit around Sage. She didn't even know if she believed in soul mates or any of that stuff. All she knew was those two were happy together and seemed great for each other.

"Be honest," Sage said. "Do you have feelings for her?"

"If you'd asked me that yesterday, my answer would have been absolutely not. After this afternoon?" Courtney sighed. "I don't want to have feelings for her. But... maybe I do."

Shit.

This was bad.

This was *very* bad.

She couldn't have romantic feelings for Vanessa. Aside from being bandmates, she would just be setting herself up for more pain and disappointment. Eventually.

Vanessa was who she was. She wouldn't settle for any one person for long, and Courtney needed commitment and stability. Even if she could forgive and trust Vanessa again—and she still wasn't sure that was even possible—they weren't a good match.

"Realizing those feelings is the important part," Sage said. "You don't have to do anything about it right now. But accepting it means you don't have to spend all your energy running around being pissed off and trying to deny it."

This was probably true. And Courtney had enough on her plate. She couldn't afford to waste energy.

She raised her glass to her lips as the server approached with two plates of blackened shrimp tacos. "You are a wise human and a fabulous friend."

"You're pretty amazing yourself," Sage said. "For now, just focus on the gigs and enjoy your comeback successes!"

"I'll try to." She leaned back so the server could place her plate in front of her. When he left, she said, "Thanks for the opportunity to do that class with you. I really enjoyed it."

"Good! I'm glad. It took a little pressure off of me, so I think that's a good partnership. No commitment. Just think of it as an option for down the road." Sage winked. "If you ever want to do something regularly, the gallery owners are great, and I think they have more times available."

"Thanks. I'll keep that in mind."

Courtney didn't want to commit to anything regular at the moment. She had enough on her plate.

And for now, she had tacos to devour.

14

VANESSA

The laundry basket was overflowing with every piece of clothing Vanessa had found strewn about the floor of her apartment and on her bed. Her bedroom had resembled a mouse nest with piles of clothes covering every surface. But it looked almost clean now.

She didn't even own a vacuum, so it wouldn't get that clean. But she could borrow one if she decided it was important. For today, this was nice. Something she should've done a long time ago.

Not that having a clean clothes basket and a dirty clothes basket wasn't an acceptable way to manage laundry. Especially when most of her wardrobe was tees and jeans and joggers. But over the last few months, her clothes weren't quite making it to either basket. So she would try this whole folding and putting away thing. For a while, at least.

She dropped the clothes near the front door, where she could grab it on her way out to run a load of laundry tomorrow. It was too late to start that now. She'd forget about it or fall asleep and leave a moldy load in the washer to find in the morning.

So she assessed the living room next.

Garrett had been right. The place was a wreck.

But she wasn't cleaning for Garrett or for anyone else. Vanessa was cleaning her apartment to kick off some kind of metaphorical and literal fresh start. An effort to have her space mirror the internal change she was pursuing.

Seeing Courtney and spending time alone with her that afternoon had done more than just captivate her attention. Talking with her had inspired hope. For their potentially rekindled friendship. For the band. For everything. Being around her made Vanessa want to do better. Whatever that meant.

Courtney was the walking, breathing definition of responsibility. She'd been taking care of her brother for years, and would no doubt look out for him long after he needed her to. Maybe she was a little obsessive about it, but Vanessa saw the love and caring that obsession filtered through and that drove it. It was endearing. Especially since Vanessa didn't have anything like that growing up.

Her parents had physically and financially taken care of her, but their actions never came from a place of love. Their caretaking stemmed from obligation. Vanessa had never felt loved or supported in that house, not how it was with Courtney and Lucas. The only family support Vanessa had ever felt came from the Danger Dames.

Nicole and Vanessa had come up with the idea for the band, and Vanessa had brought in Emily, who she'd worked with at a bar. Emily brought in Libby, and Libby brought Courtney, who she'd worked with at a restaurant in the Quarter. Those women became Vanessa's family.

And she'd gone and turned her back on them.

She sat at her tiny dinette table and tackled the stacks of junk mail and flyers and who knew what else. Most of it went straight into the trash can. She slid one paper toward the edge of the table, then snatched it before it fell off the edge. It was a flyer for a concert they'd done at this dank little bar on Chartres Street.

Vanessa smiled at the flyer and the band's name printed in the bottom right corner. It was the first time they'd gotten their names on any kind of promotional stuff. They were so brand new back then. Babies. And they were so fucking proud to see their band name in print.

The gig had been awful. The place was long closed now, and for good reason. It stank, even by French Quarter bar standards, and half the crowd left after some asshole tourist started a brawl in the middle of their second set. And they'd had to spend their measly pay buying their own beer. But it had been so worth it.

Some days, she wished she could go back to that time. Not to being a new band, but to those years when that band and her little makeshift family were her only concern. Why couldn't she have just been happy with that?

Her whole life had always been about music, and she'd been driven in pursuing new skills and leveling up. Learning new music. Searching for bigger stages. Like she always had something to prove.

She put the flyer to the side. The start of a "keep" pile. A reminder of where she'd been.

Her family had never believed in her, but the Danger Dames had. They'd built a name and a reputation and a fanbase together. They pushed each other. Lifted each other. Helped Vanessa get to the level she was at today.

She owed them her loyalty. She owed them the best Vanessa she could be.

After reaching the bottom of another stack, she landed on a folded sheet of colorful paper. Upon opening it, she recognized it as a map of the Audubon Zoo.

Another smile crept across her face.

A few months before she'd left them, the band had spent a weekday together at the zoo. Vanessa had spent most of her time in the aviary with Courtney by her side while the others split off to check out other exhibits. Vanessa had always been fascinated with birds and had been obsessed with a particular species when she was a kid.

What was it called?

All she could remember was how she used to scour the internet for pictures and checked out every library book on them she could get her hands on. She would dream about how this particular bird would be the perfect apartment pet when she grew up.

But she could only ever make enough money to pay her basic bills and rarely lived in a place that would let her have any kind of pet.

Vanessa grabbed her phone and called Nicole.

"Hey, what was that bird species I was so obsessed with as a kid?"

"Oh my gosh, Vanessa. You expect me to remember that?"

"You remember everything."

"Yeah, well, I'm not your memory assistant." A few seconds later, Nicole said, "It was some country name. Started with an 'S,' I think."

That was enough to jar the memories loose. "Senegal! Thanks!"

"Wait a second," Nicole said. "Why do you want to know?"

"It was just bugging me that I couldn't remember."

Her mind was three steps ahead, and her fingers were itching to do some research once she ended this call. But she wasn't about to let Nicole pour water on her excitement. Even if it was just excitement for what she might have a few years from now. It was nice to have dreams again. Dreams that didn't revolve solely around music.

"I don't believe you," Nicole said. "Don't forget about the gig Friday."

"I didn't forget. I'll be there," Vanessa confirmed. "Don't you forget what we talked about."

"I won't. Still don't like it, but I'll remember."

"Good," Vanessa said. "Okay, that's all. I'll see you Friday."

She hung up the phone, then looked at the last bit of papers she had to sort through. Then she glanced over at her laptop on the couch.

No. Stay on task.

She turned back to the papers and used her proposed search idea as an incentive for finishing at least what was on this table. Bird searching as a reward. She laughed at the thought and returned to cleaning.

15

COURTNEY

Courtney adjusted the mic stand while Emily plugged her into the board. The stage was exactly as she remembered, small but cozy. Just the right size for the venue. The bar was empty, but they'd come early to set up and do their soundcheck since they were all out of practice.

As Sage had suggested, Courtney planned to enjoy this gig, the opportunity to play, and the extra cash. So far, the mindset plan was working.

And she had to admit, singing on stage again would be nice. Her stomach fluttered and her mouth was dry, despite already having her pre-show tea with honey on the way here. But it felt good to have those jitters back. She'd been so worried about the past ruining everything, but this felt just like old times in a lot of ways.

Still, the time-lapse hung heavy in the air. The reason for it loomed even heavier.

To Vanessa's credit, she'd done everything right so far. She'd shown up early. She'd set up her own stuff, then helped anyone else who needed it, including helping Emily with the sound. In the past, she would have taken care of her stuff, maybe brought in an extra stand for Nicole (who usually barked at her to do so), then gone out back to text on her phone or make small talk with the bartender to warm them up for a free drink or two after the show.

This was almost a different Vanessa tonight. This Vanessa was conscientious. Present. At peace.

Time would tell if this version stuck around. Courtney wouldn't believe this change was real until she could see a new track record. Setting up for one gig wasn't proof of lasting change.

All Courtney could do was hope Vanessa would stick to her word this time. And if she couldn't, that she'd at least be honest and up front about it and be respectful enough to give them a heads up.

Nothing left to do now but watch and wait.

Vanessa finished setting up a mic stand near Nicole's drum kit and turned to catch Courtney watching her.

Shit.

It wasn't bad enough that she'd let her guard down that afternoon outside the coffee shop last week. Or that she'd confessed her feelings for Vanessa to Sage a couple days ago. Now she would have to explain why she was gawking at the woman.

Vanessa walked over with a cool, easy smile. "You all set?"

"I think so."

"Why do you look so nervous?"

Courtney twist off the cap of her water bottle and took a sip. "It's been a while since I sang in public."

"But you were great in rehearsal. This is just like that."

"With more at stake," Courtney said.

"Maybe." Vanessa shrugged. "There are always other performances, though. Try not to put so much pressure on yourself."

"Maybe for you there are other performances." She didn't mean it to sound nasty, but some of her lingering hurt had floated to the surface with those words, anyway.

Vanessa's mouth tightened, but her eyes held a look of contrition. "You're going to do great. I know it. And I've got your back. Promise."

Then Vanessa smiled and returned to her spot for their soundcheck.

Courtney's heart beat faster against her chest. Pre-performance jitters compounded by the effect of those words.

She didn't want to believe in that promise. Didn't want to suffer the inevitable hurt when it didn't pan out.

But that timid smile and those sorrowful eyes made her want to believe in Vanessa.

At least for this night.

———

"WHAT DID YOU THINK?" Nicole approached Courtney at the side of the stage, a big smug grin on her face. Not gloating, but close.

Courtney's pride didn't want to admit anything. Especially not that Nicole was right about this whole second chance for the band being a good thing.

But Sage had convinced Courtney that maybe her pride shouldn't be in charge. Not all the time, at least.

"It felt great."

Nicole's grin grew wider. "Yeah, it did." Her smile faded as she said, "Couple tunes still need work. But I'm glad we're working the kinks out here instead of at the festival."

There were a couple covers—a Fleetwood Mac one and a Joan Jett one—they hadn't rehearsed last week that were rusty tonight. But they'd pull it together by next time.

"Thanks for getting over yourself and agreeing to do this," Nicole added.

Courtney's eyes drifted to where Vanessa was packing up her cables.

She couldn't help thinking about how she had Vanessa's return to thank for this. She didn't want to be grateful, because it remained to be seen whether this change would last. But she had to admit, she wanted the change to be real. Wanted this all to be real.

Her newly recognized feelings aside, Courtney wanted her friend back.

She just wasn't ready to admit it. Not out loud. And not to Nicole.

"We all agreed to it," she said.

"Yeah, but you had the biggest objection." Nicole tilted her head and looked down her nose at Courtney. "You seem less agitated tonight. Like you're suddenly good with all of this."

"I'm not good with everything. But the gig was great. I'll admit that."

Nicole narrowed her eyes. "I've known you before today, Courtney. You don't just let shit go. You were in a better mood before we played. What gives?"

Courtney's eyes betrayed her as her gaze flicked back to Vanessa. "I ran into her the other day. We talked stuff out." She sighed and returned her attention to Nicole. "I don't trust her, but I'm willing to see what happens. And I don't have spare energy to waste fuming over what she did."

Nicole's face scrunched in surprised amusement. "I'm glad. Surprised, but glad." It was her turn to look back at Vanessa. "You know, if you want people to do better, sometimes you've got to give them a chance to do that."

Courtney nodded. "Trying."

It was one thing to admit that she was attracted to Vanessa. Seeing her and being so close to her and performing together stirred up feelings Courtney wished didn't exist. But they did. No denying that anymore.

Trusting the woman, however, was another matter. Not something she could just turn on and off. That would take time.

Time, she guessed, she was willing to put in.

"What did you think of the setlist?"

Vanessa and Courtney had always made the setlist together, but Courtney didn't have the heart to be involved with it this time. She was too afraid to get invested in something that might not pan out. The disappointment would suck no matter what, but she was trying to limit the damage.

"Seemed fine to me," she said. "Worked for this crowd."

"Hey, weren't you working on some songs before everything went south?"

Courtney hesitated. "Yeah."

"Seems with this being a regular thing, we might be able to use them." She held out an envelope. "No pressure. Just if you want to."

Courtney was already spread too thin. She didn't know where she'd pull out time to write. But the thought appealed to her, since that had been a big part of her anger over the band's breakup. She'd put so much effort into those songs. When everything fell apart, there was nothing to do with them. So they'd been sitting in a bedroom drawer for three years.

"Thanks," Courtney said, taking the envelope. Normally she'd wait to open it when she got home, since she trusted Nicole. She was better with details than all the rest of them put together. It was why she was in charge of scheduling and calls. But Courtney hadn't asked what they were getting paid, and she wondered if it was the same as last time they'd played here.

Her eyes scanned the bills inside and did a quick mental count.

"Whoa," she said. "You either worked some magic or Doug wanted us playing here again more than I guessed."

Nicole gave a tight smile that didn't quite reach her eyes. "Something like that."

Before Courtney could ask more, Vanessa appeared beside Nicole. Her cheeks were flushed, and her eyes blazed with their familiar performance high. She threw an arm over Nicole's shoulder. "Where are we going to celebrate?"

"I'm an old now," Nicole said with a scoff. "It's past my bedtime."

"Unacceptable," said Vanessa. "That was too good not to acknowledge."

Courtney fought to hold her tongue. She wanted to agree, but she was still guarding her words. And her heart, she supposed.

Nicole could sense something, however, and was peering at her through narrowed eyes. "I could stick around here a little longer, I guess."

Vanessa squeezed her neck and kissed her cousin's cheek with a squeal.

"*One* round," Nicole insisted. "That's it."

Vanessa released her grip and held her hands in the air. "Heard and understood."

"I'm gonna load the rest of the sound equipment," Nicole said.

Vanessa gave a salute as Nicole left, then turned to Courtney, a smile still plastered across her face. Courtney felt drawn to her like a moth that was incapable of learning its lesson.

"Thanks for giving me another chance." There was an uncharacteristic rawness in Vanessa's words.

Courtney shrugged. "You deserved a second chance."

"Yeah, but you didn't have to give one to me." Vanessa held Courtney's gaze. The sincerity in her tone was almost unbearable. "I just want you to know I appreciate it."

Something about that kind of honesty and vulnerability coming from Vanessa made Courtney want to pull her in and hold her close. Give her every reason to stick around this time.

But no. Vanessa had to prove they could trust her. With no added incentive or desperate pleading from any of them.

Courtney managed a nod of acknowledgment and kept her traitorous mouth shut.

Vanessa gestured at the bar. "Can I buy you a drink? Gin and tonic? Or something different these days?"

Courtney's body heated with the realization that Vanessa had remembered her post-performance drink of choice. Just like the tea. It had only been three years, but she'd surely learned dozens of drink preferences since then. Courtney had expected hers would have faded into the background. Dull and unimportant.

But maybe she wasn't so unimportant to Vanessa after all.

"Yeah, the same still."

Vanessa smiled brightly, a hint of pride in her eyes. Although it was unclear whether it was pride in her memory or pride in being responsible for the flush now hitting Courtney's cheeks.

Dammit.

This had better be a quick drink or Courtney would be a goner.

16

VANESSA

Vanessa drummed her fingers on the bar while she stared at the bottles lining the shelves, counting them one by one to recenter her thoughts and slow everything way the fuck down.

It wasn't her fault. It was that fucking *look* in Courtney's eyes. The one where she was looking right through Vanessa, peering into her soul. It had always made Vanessa itchy, but she'd chalked it up to not wanting to be looked at.

No, that was a lie. Vanessa loved being noticed. She knew she was attractive, no point pretending otherwise for modesty's sake. She looked good, so she fucking owned it.

But she didn't like people seeing beneath that. Her insides were... less attractive.

So Courtney looking at her that way always raised Vanessa's walls.

But now... now they were a different defense. Now, those walls were up because part of Vanessa wanted to let Courtney in. Wanted to let her see every part of her.

And that absolutely couldn't happen.

Or could it?

"On the house," the tall, juicy bartender said as he slid a gin and tonic and a whiskey sour her way. Too bad he was off the menu tonight.

She winked her thanks and carried the drinks to where Courtney sat with the rest of the band.

Thank goodness they wouldn't be sitting in a booth alone. Vanessa wasn't sure she could sit here alone with Courtney and not blurt out something she might regret.

She'd forgotten how much of a high playing with this group was. Sure, she loved playing, no matter who she was with. But there was a musical synergy between these women that was better than anything else. Vanessa could kick herself for ever leaving. She didn't know why she had.

Okay, that was another lie.

She knew why she'd left.

Ego and desire.

Garrett had done a masterful job of stroking her ego until he'd gotten what he'd wanted from her—on stage and off—then grew bored. And the desire part... that was her own damn fault. She'd had big dreams. Big dreams that band wouldn't help her reach. They all had too many other priorities. None of them wanted it as much as she did. Damn if she even knew what "it" was. Something bigger and better.

But nothing had ever matched the feeling she got playing with these people.

Vanessa set a plastic cup on the table, startling Courtney. She looked up, her eyes fluttering as if waking up to Vanessa's face. Waking up from a long night together, with the sun peeking through the shade late in the morning...

Holy shit. Vanessa needed to get a grip on her brain.

"Thanks." Courtney's voice was husky from a night of singing lead.

Emily raised her glass the second Vanessa's butt hit the bench. "To us all back together again!"

Her words were slurred and her eyes glassy. She'd clearly downed a shot or two after the show.

Vanessa held out her hand. "Babe, keys."

It was a reflex. Like old times when any of them got out of hand. Sometimes a night would get away from them, especially after a good performance.

"I drove us." Libby held up her plastic cup of dark liquid. "Just Coke."

Vanessa relaxed a little and slid into the only empty spot next to Courtney. Their arms pressed against each other, and Vanessa resisted the urge to spread out and touch her knee to Courtney's. Her whole body was vibrating with the sensation of their shoulders touching. She was convinced she'd keel over right there if she came into contact with any other part of this woman.

She shook her head, bringing her mind back to the conversation, but realized Courtney was looking at her. Studying her.

"What?"

As if caught doing something she shouldn't, Courtney flinched and turned away, snatching her drink. "Nothing."

That wasn't nothing. But Vanessa decided not to press the issue with a full audience across from them.

That was when she realized the three of them had squeezed in on the opposite side to force Vanessa and Courtney to share the other side. Nicole's shit-eating grin confirmed it.

"Are you all going to just leave me hanging here?" Emily slurred even more, this time sloshing her drink in the air for emphasis.

"Shit, sorry." Vanessa lifted her cup, as did the others, and they met above the table's center.

"To just like the old days," Libby said.

Vanessa felt Courtney tense beside her, and without even looking, she could feel Nicole's eyes lasering in on her.

"How about to new times?" Vanessa offered.

Libby smiled. "Even better."

"To new times!" the group said in near unison.

But one voice was softer than the rest.

Vanessa couldn't blame her for any hesitancy. She'd have to earn Courtney's confidence. And that would take time. Time that more of these gigs would give her.

And Vanessa could be patient. Sure, it wasn't her strong suit, but she could do it if she tried. And there was a good reason for it. Courtney was the best reason.

She took a big gulp of her whiskey sour and struggled to remember what the fuck she was doing here.

It was Courtney's arm against hers that did the reminding.

She was here to play music. And she now had a new goal: to win Courtney's trust.

And maybe her affection, too.

Damn. The bartender must have put in an extra shot because her brain was turning muddy.

Or was that Courtney turning her brain muddy?

"We didn't get a chance to catch up yet," Libby said. "What have you been up to?"

Vanessa didn't want to get into her relationship or band history right now. And as she'd concluded recently, there wasn't much else to her life. But she had one bit of conversation starter.

"I'm getting a bird."

She felt Courtney's gaze on her. Vanessa was too afraid to check if the look came with interest or judgment.

"I thought you were just reminiscing or some shit," Nicole said. "I wouldn't have answered that question if

I knew you were gonna run out and buy one of the damn things on a whim."

"It wasn't on a whim." Not exactly. "I don't have it yet."

"What kind?" Emily asked. "Ooh, is it one of those big green ones? Or just one of those little blue things?"

Vanessa pulled out her phone and showed them the photo from the Westbank Animal Warriors' website. Even she had to admit, this wasn't the best look for the guy. He was missing quite a bit of feathers —from stress and not illness, the shelter had assured her. She used her hand to cover his bio beneath the photo. It wasn't super flattering either.

Emily and Libby both cooed at the image, while Nicole looked down her nose and scowled.

"That thing looks like it makes a mess. You're a mess all by yourself. How are you gonna take care of that?"

"Who's going to take care of it when you're out of town?" Courtney asked.

Ah. So it was a judgmental look, not interested or amused. Good to know Vanessa still had a lot of work ahead of her. Clearly, a bird wouldn't win Courtney over. Not on its own.

Fine. She liked a challenge.

"I told you. I'm not playing with anyone else. So unless you all go on tour, I won't be leaving him."

"He still looks like a mess," Nicole repeated.

"Maybe. But I'm capable of cleaning." Vanessa

stirred her drink while they continued to look at her phone. "You should see my apartment."

Nicole grunted. "I've *seen* your apartment."

"You should see it now. I cleaned it."

Nicole eyed her suspiciously but said nothing else.

Emily grabbed the phone in Vanessa's hand and aimed it at Courtney. "Look how cute he is!"

Courtney glanced at the photo. Her mouth remained taut and her eyes were filled with doubt. "He is cute. Looks like he's had a rough patch, but cute."

"He's *adorable*," Emily insisted.

"He's stressed from the move," Vanessa said, scrambling for anything that might help inspire confidence and ease Courtney's doubt. "The shelter said his feathers should all grow back once he's settled and feels safe again."

Courtney's phone rang on the table. She snatched it and answered in one harried motion. "What's wrong?"

They all went silent and waited for more. Vanessa stiffened and held her breath.

It had to be Lucas.

"I'm on my way." Courtney ended the call and scooted sideways.

Vanessa hurried to clear a path out of the booth. "Is he okay?"

"Yeah. No." Courtney shook her head, stumbling over each word. "I'm not sure. I need to pick him up."

"Let me drive you." Vanessa dug for her keys and

caught sight of her empty whiskey cup. "Or call you a ride?"

"I'm fine." Courtney put her phone in her pocket. "I hardly drank anything."

A quick glance at the full cup of clear liquid where Courtney had been sitting confirmed she'd only been taking slow, small sips of her drink.

"I can ride with you." When that didn't seem to sit well either, Vanessa said, "Or walk you to your car."

"I'm just down the street not far. I got here early."

Vanessa didn't want to let her leave like this, but if Courtney didn't want help or company, Vanessa couldn't force it down her throat.

"Call us when you know more," Nicole said. "Let me know if we can do anything, and if y'all are okay."

Courtney nodded and gave a half-hearted wave. "I will."

Then she disappeared into the crowd.

There was an awkward silence despite the blaring music over the speakers. Vanessa was still standing beside the booth, unable to make her feet move. She should sit back down with the group, but she was afraid if she put any energy into her leg muscles, they might chase after Courtney instead.

A surefire way to piss off Courtney would be to not respect her wishes. And, at this moment, she wished to handle whatever this was alone.

"Well, that would have sobered me up if I wasn't already," Libby said.

Emily slid out of the booth. "I have to pee."

"I'll go with you," Libby said.

Vanessa sat across from Nicole, who she now realized was staring her down. "What?"

"Ease up there, speed racer."

"What are you talking about?"

"I've known you our whole lives. Long enough to know when you've got a thing for someone." Nicole shook her head. "And Courtney isn't just someone."

Was it that obvious?

Vanessa nodded at Nicole's empty cup. "I thought you said only one drink? You aren't making sense."

"I'm making perfect sense," Nicole said. "You're the one who needs a dose of sense here."

"I still don't know what you're talking about." Vanessa leaned against the back of the booth bench and avoided eye contact.

Nicole scoffed. "Okay, we can play that game if you want. You don't need me to tell you not to fuck this up again."

"I'm not fucking anything up," Vanessa insisted. "I told you. I'm getting a bird."

"Ah yes, this magical bird." Nicole laughed and drained the last of whatever was in her cup. "Just take things slow. Okay? Courtney's got enough shit going on. She doesn't need added drama."

"Oh, I'm drama now?" When Nicole raised a brow at her, Vanessa said, "I'm not fucking anything up."

"You don't intend to, but you're blazing in like you

do with everything else. And Courtney isn't everything else."

"I know that," she said through gritted teeth.

"Just remember it, okay? That woman's been through enough of people dipping out of her life and having to clean up the mess. Just promise me you'll take it slow and not leave another mess for her."

"I told you, I cleaned my apartment. I'm done with messes."

"Just promise me," Nicole said. "Slow."

There was no point denying it anymore. Nicole always could read her better than anyone else.

As much as Vanessa didn't like being told what to do, it was comforting to have someone in her corner and know someone was watching for when she might screw this up.

Because Nicole was right. She really didn't want to screw this up.

Vanessa drew a cross over her heart with one finger. "I promise."

17

COURTNEY

AFTER EXECUTING THE WORST PARALLEL PARKING job of her life, Courtney dashed out of her car and toward the bright blue lights. A cop sat behind the driver's seat with his head down. An ambulance was parked along the road, and Courtney's heart sank as she spotted Lucas sitting on the curb, holding something pressed against the back of his skull.

"Oh, my God. Are you bleeding?" She did a quick head-to-toe visual evaluation. "Are you hurt anywhere else?"

"I'm fine," he insisted. "Calm down. I'm okay. They just wouldn't let me drive on my own."

Courtney looked at the attractive brunette standing beside him in a paramedic uniform. "How much is he lying?"

The young woman smiled and stuffed her hands in her jacket pockets. It was the first cool night they'd had of this early fall season, but it barely registered in Courtney's brain. She had no interest in enjoying it the way she normally would.

"He took a blow to the back of the head, but there's no bleeding. He says he didn't lose consciousness and is refusing a ride to the E.R."

Courtney smacked her brother on the arm. "Why didn't you go to the hospital?"

"Ow!" Laughter accompanied his protest. "Um, hello... injured here."

"Not enough to knock some sense into you, apparently."

"Megan said I didn't have to."

"I said we couldn't legally force him to get checked out if he refused, but I recommended he call for a ride and have someone to monitor his condition overnight."

Courtney mouthed *thank you* to the paramedic, then returned her attention to her stubborn little brother. "I can drive you to the hospital if you don't want to take the ambulance."

"No way. Do you know what an E.R. visit costs? I told you, I'm fine."

Courtney turned to Megan again and waited for confirmation.

"We checked him out. He looks okay." Megan looked down at Lucas. "I'd recommend keeping him awake for a while and continuing to apply ice on and off for the swelling. Monitor for any additional symptoms, and if he develops nausea, vomiting, or a headache beyond localized soreness, go immediately to an emergency room."

"Thank you." Courtney exhaled and urged her heart to beat again. "Do I need to sign off on anything?"

Megan shook her head. "He already signed the transport refusal form."

Right. Because he's an adult now.

Sort of.

Megan's partner waved her over from the front of the ambulance, and she looked at Lucas with a stern expression that told Courtney the paramedic had already dealt with his bullshit before Courtney arrived.

"Keep ice on that." Megan turned to Courtney and smiled. "I hope you both have a better rest of the evening."

Courtney thanked her again, noting her brother's voice was lower than normal as he did the same.

"She was cute."

"No, we're not doing this," he said.

A car door closed behind them, and Courtney turned to find a policeman approaching with a clipboard.

"Did you give your statement already?"

Lucas nodded and kept silent as the cop approached. While Courtney wasn't particularly fond of cops herself, her brother held an even greater distrust of them. He'd witnessed several of his friends and classmates getting hassled and even arrested for petty bullshit, while the violent crimes of the city sat unsolved in their files.

Courtney had a feeling this incident would go the same direction. She was glad Lucas wanted to keep quiet as much as possible. Better than running his mouth and ending up in trouble himself.

After the cop finished his paperwork, he gave Lucas his card to call if he thought of anything he needed to add to his statement. Lucas stood and put the card in his back pocket, frowning as the cop returned to his car, turned off his lights, and left.

"Yeah, right. Like I'm going to waste my time. That would be as useless as he is."

Courtney ignored the statement in favor of her more pressing concern. "Are you dizzy at all?"

"No. Just tired."

"Well, too bad. You can't sleep," she said. "Cute medic's orders."

"You're going to enjoy bossing me all night, aren't you?"

"Better believe it." Courtney wrapped her arm around his, more to hold herself upright than worrying about him. The kid was a tree. Steady and rooted.

Except he wasn't a kid anymore. He'd signed his own care refusal and had given a statement to the police without her help. He'd handled his business.

But what if this had gone some other way? What if this had been worse somehow?

They walked together to her car, and she released

her grip on his arm so he could get in the passenger's side.

"I could have walked home."

"Do you want me to call that cute medic back to explain again why not?"

He gave a sly grin. "Maybe?"

Courtney rolled her eyes and started the car. "I knew I shouldn't have let you walk home from work."

She would be kicking herself for weeks about sticking around for a drink instead of packing up the second that gig was over. He'd convinced her he would be okay, but he was eighteen. Risk doesn't exist when you're eighteen.

"Sorry you had to leave early."

"I was done," she said.

She should have been done before she sat in that booth. She should have been done the second Vanessa's arm touched hers and sent shock waves through her body.

But no. She had to stick around for the whole group bonding and unity thing.

Who was she kidding? She'd stuck around for Vanessa as much as anything. It had initially annoyed her when the other band members strategically crammed on one side of the booth, leaving the other side open for her and Vanessa. But part of her had been giddy to be so close.

That part of her, however, shouldn't get a say.

What this night was teaching her was that she

couldn't divide her focus any further. She was already spread too thin. Sure, Lucas seemed okay tonight. But what about next time? A relationship would only distract her from what was most important.

He put the cold pack in his lap and winced as he rested his head against the seat.

Courtney pulled out onto the road. "I should still drive you to get checked out."

"I'm fine," he said. "Just sore. I'll feel worse if we get a big bill for nothing."

"Don't worry about the money."

"We have to worry about the money. Isn't that what you always say?"

"I'm talking about concerts and bar tabs, not hospital visits when you need them. That's the stuff I save for. To make sure we can pay these bills."

"But it's still better if we don't have to pay them."

"Oh, speaking of money." She made sure her envelope was in the cupholder, and she hadn't forgotten it back at the bar. "I'm getting paid more than I thought for these gigs. So if you can take care of your expenses, and I can do well this fall and holiday season, we can build up our emergency fund even more."

"I thought you were going to say we could do more concerts and bar tabs."

"Har har," she said. "What it means is go to the fucking doctor if you need to."

It also meant no panic attacks if the car needed a minor repair or anything like that. All she wanted was some financial breathing room. An extra fifty bucks a week wouldn't make them rich, but it would at least cover a couple of Lucas's therapy sessions.

"I guess this is the part where I thank you for being all responsible and shit."

"No need," she said. "I just want you safe and healthy."

If that meant skipping future post-gig drinks to pick him up, she'd gladly do that from now on.

"Well, thanks anyway. For being responsible and for picking me up. And for, you know, caring and shit."

The kid deserved someone who cared about him. She wished her mom had given him that, and not just because things would have been easier on Courtney. She wished that because it would have been easier on him. Knowing their mom had chosen to leave did a number on him, even if he tried to deny it. So she would do her best to make sure he understood she had his back, no matter what.

"So tell me the whole story," she said. "What happened?"

"There's no story. I was texting Malcolm, then I got hit from behind. Someone grabbed my wallet and ran."

"Dang it, Lucas. Didn't I tell you to pay attention and not play on your phone when you're walking around at night?"

"I thought that was just shit girls were supposed to worry about."

Courtney burned red hot and exhaled. "Seriously?"

"Sorry," he said. "I didn't have much cash on me. Maybe twenty bucks. But I'll have to get a new license. Oh, and I already canceled my credit card. Megan suggested that while we were waiting for you."

At least that was taken care of. The license wasn't a huge deal. More of an inconvenience.

"Were you able to give the police a description of the person?"

"Did you not hear the part about me getting smacked in the head from behind?"

"I'm asking if you saw them run away," she said. "Since you told the paramedics you didn't lose consciousness, right?"

"Nope." He fiddled with the cold pack resting on his leg. "I mean, I didn't pass out on the ground or anything. I guess I was in shock or whatever."

"Mmhmm."

She wasn't letting him doze off any time soon. He probably had a minor concussion. But she knew enough first aid to know what signs to watch for. She would just have to look up how long to keep him awake. At least she didn't have any obligations tomorrow, since she'd planned to be tired from the gig, anyway. She'd stay up all night and sleep in, then get to work casting later in the day.

"I told you, I'm fine."

She glanced sideways at him once she stopped at a

red light. "I really am glad you're okay. You scared the shit out of me tonight."

"I'm sorry."

"Don't be. It's what I'm here for. To worry about you and to be here when you need me. I just need you to be safe."

"I know," he said. "And I promise I won't text while I'm walking at night anymore."

"Well, you won't, because I'm picking you up after every night shift from now on."

"Court, you don't—"

"I don't want to hear it. I get to boss you all night, remember?"

He laughed, and she could tell the motion hurt more than he let on.

"All right, all right," he said. "But can we pick up a Coke and some seasoned fries? I'll need energy for this marathon bossing session."

The light turned green, and Courtney made a right-hand turn to swing by his favorite place. "Deal."

18

VANESSA

A BRUNETTE WITH A MESSY PONYTAIL AND A Westbank Animal Warriors T-shirt met Vanessa in the little gravel parking lot. She waited near the welcome sign and waved as she rocked back and forth on her heels.

"Hi, I'm Molly." She extended her hand. "Vanessa?"

She shook Molly's hand. "Yeah. I'm here about Bob."

"Right." The woman lit up at that. "We were hoping we'd find just the right person for him."

"Hopefully that's me."

Molly's expression dropped a little. "Our one big concern is that you've never had a bird before. And Bob is... well, you did read his bio, right?"

Vanessa had read it. Multiple times. Initially in

disbelief, then whenever she needed a giggle. "I did. I think he's absolutely perfect."

"It's just that he's not exactly a beginner's bird," Molly said. "This place isn't suited for him to stay long, and we don't have any bird foster homes to send him to. Especially not any without kids or pets or... men."

Vanessa suppressed a laugh. That had been Bob's main issue in his previous home, and the reason he couldn't remain with his original family. He hated the owner's husband and had an epic bite. Rather than keeping him caged and having the wife be the only one who could ever feed or clean him, the owners had decided to see if the shelter could find Bob another home.

"No men at my place," Vanessa said. "And if he works as ex repellant, all the better."

Molly bit her lip and smiled, obviously trying to keep her response professional. But it was clear she might know a thing or two about shitty exes deserving a parrot bite.

"Aside from his distaste for men, Bob really is a sweetheart. He isn't much of a talker, though. Mostly clucks and whistles. The good news is he isn't very squawky either."

Vanessa's neighbors would appreciate that. But she already knew Senegals were a quieter parrot.

"I've done a lot of research on Sennies," Vanessa said. "I was kind of obsessed with them as a kid."

Most kids had a favorite breed of cat or dog.

Vanessa had a favorite parrot species. She enjoyed standing out by being into something different from everyone else. But also, she just really liked those birds.

"So you know he'll need lots of interaction time." Molly looked concerned again. "Your application said you're a musician?"

"That's right."

"Do you have someone to care for him when you're away? Because they'll need to also be introduced and have plenty of interaction time with the other person before you're gone for the first time."

Vanessa shook her head. "I won't be on the road."

The words were harder to force out than she expected. She'd liked being able to say she was a touring musician. It was an ego thing, and she wasn't too proud to admit it.

Molly relaxed a little. "I'm glad to hear you'll have plenty of time to bond. Ready to meet him?"

"Dying to."

Vanessa followed Molly inside the building and down a narrow hallway.

"We're keeping his cage in the director's room, but he hasn't taken to anyone enough to get much free time yet. We have a lot of trouble getting him back inside. And with all the animals coming in and out of this building and the noise of that, this isn't an ideal situation for him." Molly opened the office door and led the way to a large black metal cage occupying an entire corner of the room. "He might be a little cranky and take some time to warm up once you get him home."

"I know the feeling." Vanessa crossed the room and stood in front of the cage with her hands behind her back, far from the bars.

Bob was a gorgeous green color, with a gray head and bright orange belly. He looked better in person than in his photo, and most of his missing feathers were growing back. A good sign that he'd been receiving excellent care here, despite the staff not having much experience with birds.

He tilted his head one way and then the other, examining her in return. After he finished his assessment, he made soft chattering noises and clucks.

"Aww. He likes you already."

Vanessa smiled at the bird. "Same, pal."

"Now, I have to warn you. Bob isn't a morning bird."

Vanessa turned and laughed at that. "Poor guy can't have coffee, so that's understandable."

"He gets a little crabby if you let him out or try to interact too early. So I'd wait to do any cage cleaning or to let him out until later in the day."

"I'm not much of a morning person either, so it sounds like we'll get along fine."

"Great! Do you want me to get the paperwork for you?"

"Yes, definitely."

Molly clapped softly. "Excellent. We'll start out

with a foster-to-adopt contract, and I'll check in with you to see how things are going. Then we can finalize everything after about a month. Does that sound good?"

"Sounds great," Vanessa said. "His bio said his adoption fee includes his cage?"

"Sure does. Do you have a vehicle you can take him home in today?"

Vanessa always had instruments or extra band-mates to schlep around, so she had plenty of space in her jeep for this cage.

When she confirmed that, Molly said she'd be right back with the forms and slipped out of the room.

All alone with her new friend, Vanessa had an instant moment of regret.

She wasn't one to struggle with making decisions or with second-guessing them. But ever since the night of that gig, a week ago yesterday, she couldn't let go of the look Courtney had when she'd heard about the bird. The look that had implied Courtney thought this would be yet another thing Vanessa would drop the ball on. The look that stung more than any words could.

Vanessa had found out the next day from Nicole that Lucas was okay. After that, Vanessa stopped worrying about them and resumed obsessing about Courtney's lack of faith in her.

But Vanessa had every intention of following

through on this. She wanted to give this bird a second chance with her.

Only... what if good intentions weren't enough? What if she *couldn't* give this guy everything he needed? What if she got bored the way she always did? She couldn't just abandon him like a worn-out hobby.

No. She *wouldn't*.

She'd wanted a bird like this for as long as she could remember. And, if she was being super honest with herself, she was pretty lonely in that apartment.

Plus, this was a perfect opportunity to prove to Courtney that she'd changed. That this bird and the band—and maybe one day Courtney—could count on Vanessa to stick by them.

There was just one thing standing in her way.

Vanessa took a step back and assessed the cage. With the legs unscrewed, she was pretty sure it would fit in her jeep. And Molly would help her put it in there. But she had no idea how she would get Bob inside her apartment.

19

COURTNEY

"Which one?"

Courtney held up two resin ornaments—a blue fairy and a green dinosaur with a Santa hat—which dangled from clear fishing line hooked on her fingers. Sage tilted her head side to side, considering the options from her seat on the couch.

"Both?" Sage bit her lip, like the choice pained her. "But if you make me choose, that t-rex is adorable."

"That's what I said." Lucas walked past them into the kitchen, where he grabbed an orange soda from the fridge. "It's like she thinks I have no taste or something."

"I just want to make sure that concussion didn't blur your senses." She winked at him so he knew she was joking. He'd been the one to start with the jokes the night of the assault. Jokes that lots of people might find inappropriate or insensitive, but they'd learned to laugh at a lot of things over the years. She liked to think their little inside jokes, even the ones at their own expense, kept them close besides releasing some pressure once in a while.

And it helped that it had been just over a week since he'd gotten the injury, so Courtney could breathe a little easier that he was past any scary concussion effects at this point. He wasn't suffering from headaches or pain or anything, and he'd gone back to work two days after with no problems. The only lingering effect of the incident was Courtney's worsening insomnia.

She wasn't worried about that happening again. Part of her brain was rational enough to know that he didn't work in a dangerous area, and she was picking him up after his shifts for now. It had just been a random mugging, a thing that could have happened to him any time, any place with some bad luck.

But another less rational part of her brain spun every night on all the other random things that could happen to Lucas. And the less sleep she got, the less capable she was of using her tools and helping herself get back to sleep.

"My senses could see that the dinosaur looks better," Lucas said. "Maybe you're the one who was concussed?"

"I think I'd remember that," she said.

"Or would you?"

They both laughed, but Courtney realized Sage was still considering something.

"My gut says that one, if we have to pick just one. I know fairies are kind of your thing, though. Honestly, either is a good choice."

Courtney looked at them again. "I think your gut was right with both. I think I can make it work and bring both sets of molds."

She'd enjoyed making these test items and was even coming around to glitter. She still preferred working with metal, but these resin projects were growing on her. So was teaching. Courtney didn't know where that might lead, but she was enjoying these two classes for now and was grateful to her friend for setting her up with the opportunity.

Her phone vibrated on the kitchen counter near Lucas. He held it up and waved it to see if Courtney wanted him to bring it over.

"Who is it?"

Lucas looked at the screen and cringed. "I don't want to say."

"Then how am I supposed to know if I want to answer it?"

He looked back down at the phone, still hesitating. "It's Vanessa."

Her heart rate kicked up a notch while a pit opened in her stomach. How could one woman stir up so many conflicting emotions?

Courtney considered letting it ring. She could deal

with the voice mail if it was important enough to require one.

Then again, she'd have to deal with the voice mail eventually, so she might as well get this over with, right?

But maybe answering Vanessa's call in front of Lucas and Sage, who would both analyze her every word and breath, wasn't in her best interest.

Courtney held out her hand, and Lucas hurried over with the phone. Then he sat on the couch beside Sage where they both stared at her, waiting with nosy anticipation.

"Hello?"

"Hey, Courtney." Vanessa's voice was, as usual, loud, confident, and upbeat. "This is going to be a weird ask, but Nicole isn't answering, and I backed myself in a bit of a corner here."

Backing herself into a corner with no forethought was kind of Vanessa's thing. But it wasn't like Courtney would hang up on someone who needed her help. Not even Vanessa.

Maybe even especially Vanessa.

"Just ask," Courtney said.

"Well..." There was an awkward hesitation and what sounded like a whistle in the background. "I was wondering if you could spare a few minutes to help me get a bird into my apartment."

Courtney must have misheard that. "I'm sorry, what?"

"I adopted a bird. Remember the one I showed y'all after the gig the other night?"

Right. The one she showed them right before Courtney got Lucas's call. Made sense that she'd forgotten all about it after what happened next.

But now Courtney remembered what she'd thought of that bird. Yes, it had been cute. It also looked like a lot of work and responsibility. She'd assumed Vanessa would have either grown bored with the idea or realized the downsides before finalizing anything. Apparently, animal adoptions moved faster than Courtney guessed they would. And faster than Vanessa's boredom this time.

"You want me to help you move a bird," she repeated.

"I'll help!" Lucas jumped to his feet. He'd always had a massive crush on Vanessa. Now that Courtney was looking at her old friend with a slightly different perspective, she couldn't blame him. But she sure as hell wouldn't encourage it.

She pointed at the couch and mouthed, *sit down*.

"If you're still at the same house, my new apartment isn't far from you. I'm in Westbank right now, but my place is in St. Roch. If you have a minute, I can meet you there in half an hour, unload this, and have you on your way a few minutes later."

Courtney processed all of that and did a gut check, just like Sage had taught her. She listened to her inner voice, the one that usually defaulted to *no* and needed a good reason for a yes. If the person involved was someone she deeply cared about, that was a good enough reason. Lucas was always a yes. Sage had become a yes.

But nothing about this would benefit the people closest to her. There was no good reason to put herself in Vanessa's presence again. No good reason to subject herself to the inner turmoil from sharing the same air and picking at old scabs.

No good reason except that Vanessa had asked for help.

"Send me the address."

She caught the grins Lucas and Sage exchanged. If she didn't know any better, she'd think they had something to do with setting this up.

But they couldn't have had anything to do with Vanessa adopting a bird without a plan.

"Great! Thanks. I'll text the address and load him up to meet you there in about thirty minutes."

Courtney tossed the phone on the couch between Sage and Lucas and turned to walk down the hall.

"I can go with you," Lucas offered.

"You're staying here and finishing that history paper," she called over her shoulder. "I'm going to the bathroom, and I won't be gone long. She's not far from here."

Sage stood and grabbed her tote bag. "My work here is done anyway, so I'll get out of your hair. Unless you could use an extra set of hands with that bird?"

147

She'd been so flustered by her calm response to helping Vanessa that she'd forgotten about her guest.

"I think we'll be fine," she said. "Sorry, I'll walk you out."

"I can find the exit." Sage laughed, nodding at the kitchen door just a few yards away. "Go do what you need to. Let me know how it goes. Oh, and I want bird pics!"

Courtney rolled her eyes. "You want Vanessa pics."

"Why not both?" Sage winked. "See you later. Have fun!"

Courtney shook her head as the door closed behind Sage. Her phone dinged a moment after with Vanessa's address.

"Sure I can't come with you? I can finish the paper after." Lucas paused and added, "Unless you don't want me cramping your style?"

Courtney ignored him and headed to the bathroom. Not certain how to even answer that question for herself.

20

VANESSA

After another glance down the road, Vanessa checked the time on her phone again. Based on the timing of the "on my way" text and her memory of how far away Courtney's place in the Bywater was, Courtney would arrive any second.

Vanessa bit the skin around her thumbnail. A habit Garrett hated, which made her want to do it even more out of spite. But Vanessa's fingers didn't appreciate it either, and she couldn't play her guitar with bandages, so she'd tried to kick the habit. She was more on than off with it lately.

The bird whistled and clucked at her, which was most of his vocabulary so far. She looked at him and back at her nails. Now that she had him, she had an actual reason to stop putting her fingers in her mouth. Sure, she'd still need to wash her hands more regularly, but chewing her nails and fingers would carry extra risk now with his germs in the mix.

Vanessa needed a different nervous habit. Something besides the pacing she was already doing.

She hadn't expected Courtney to come over and help. They hadn't reached the "forgive and forget" stage of repairing their friendship yet, and if someone who'd hurt her had asked for a favor, Vanessa would have laughed and hung up.

More proof that Courtney was too good for this world. Definitely proof that she'd never be interested in a relationship with someone as petty and careless as Vanessa.

No, that was the old Vanessa. New Vanessa had a bird and responsibilities. She would prove that.

Who was she kidding? She couldn't even prove to herself that she could stop biting her damn fingers.

She spit a piece of skin onto the curb as a silver sedan approached. After completing a perfect parallel parking job, Courtney exited the car. Half of her blonde bob was pulled back in a clip, leaving loose strands framing her face. She wore a faded, granite-colored Wonder Woman T-shirt and high wasted light wash jeans.

"Thanks for coming."

"Sure." Courtney gave a small nod at Vanessa's jeep. "I guess that's him?"

"Meet Bob."

Courtney laughed. "Bob?"

"Yup. That's the name he came with. And he had it for a bunch of years with the previous owner, so there's no changing it."

Courtney smiled at the grumpy-looking bird on his perch. "It kind of fits him."

"I think so," Vanessa said. "Want to help grab him? I don't want to hold you up."

"I'm not in a rush." She looked for a second like her own words had shocked her, or as if she wished she hadn't said them. "But I'm sure he wants out of there."

Vanessa showed Courtney where to grab the cage from underneath so Bob couldn't reach her fingers. Bob, however, wasn't interested in anything but judging them while they struggled to slide his cage out of Vanessa's jeep.

They carried it up the porch steps and into Vanessa's newly cleaned apartment. Then they placed the cage on Vanessa's dinette table, where she decided he would live for a bit until she could let him out and screw the legs back on the bottom.

"Well, I'll leave you two to get acquainted."

"You don't have to leave," Vanessa said. "Can I get you something to drink? Soda? Tea? Something harder? Or let me order some dinner. I owe you for helping me with this thing."

Courtney smiled at the flurry of words falling out of Vanessa's mouth. "You don't owe me anything." She looked back at the bird. "A friend of mine asked to see him. Can I take a photo?"

"Yeah, sure. If you let me order food for you? Or we can walk down to Simeon's Seafood. Oh my gosh, have you eaten there? They have this amazing crawfish poutine on the menu now."

"You really—"

"I insist. A photo in exchange for free food. Those are my terms."

Please, please, please take them.

Courtney chewed on the inside of her mouth. That nervous little gesture grew more adorable every time Vanessa caught sight of it.

"I don't know. I told Lucas I wouldn't be long."

"I'll send food for him, too. I'm guessing he'd rather that than you home early."

"You guess correctly." Courtney laughed. "Okay. Let me text to make sure."

"Whatever you guys want, I'll place the order." She made kissing noises at Bob while Courtney texted, and the bird clucked and kissed back. "How's Lucas doing? Nicole said he was robbed or something?"

Courtney finished sending her text. "Got hit in the head from behind and his wallet was stolen, but he's fine now. I never should have let him walk home from work so late and alone."

Vanessa wanted a word in a dark alley with whoever hurt that kid. He'd hung around so many of their rehearsals in the early days, it felt a bit like he was her little brother too. Or maybe a little cousin. She didn't know the guy very well, but she still felt protective of him.

"Glad he's okay. But you shouldn't beat yourself up. He's kind of getting past the age where you have a say in that kind of stuff."

Courtney gave a stubborn pout that made Vanessa want to cross the room and nibble on that lip.

"I'm picking him up from work from now on. I'll have to head straight there as soon as gigs are over if he's working those nights."

Vanessa could see the guilt eating at her. No amount of repeating that it wasn't Courtney's fault would erase that guilt. Vanessa knew her well enough to know that. But she had to do something. And not just as payment for helping with Bob. That look of guilt was tearing at her insides.

But the only way Vanessa could help right now was to feed Courtney. And maybe distract her for a little while. If she could convince Courtney to take her offer.

Courtney's phone dinged, and she laughed. "He asked if I could pick up from Simeon's on my way home."

Vanessa's heart raced as she begged it to settle down and pace itself for once. Nicole was right. She needed to take things slowly with Courtney. She was still on edge from her brother's assault and in overprotective mode. That meant she'd scare off if Vanessa pushed too hard too soon.

Or worse.

Vanessa could manage flight. She could be patient. Reel Courtney back in if needed.

But fight? Vanessa did not want to trigger that reflex. They'd end up right back where they'd picked up a month ago. At each other's throats with hurt and frustration and resentment. They'd come too far now to go back to that. She refused to go back to that. Not when there was so much potential in front of them.

"Then it's a unanimous decision." Vanessa grabbed her keys and bag. "Ready when you are."

21

COURTNEY

Simeon's Seafood was bustling even though it wasn't quite normal dinner hours yet. The place was far enough from the Quarter and Bourbon and nestled on the edge of a residential area, but it was surrounded by short-term rentals that brought in an all-hours touristy crowd. But they had a loyal local base and served up dishes that New Orleans natives gobbled up and recommended to each other.

The decor was simple—glossy wooden tables and bar, white walls and columns with windows that opened up to let in a breeze and conversations from the sidewalks outside. They picked a table near an open window, and a server arrived almost immediately to bring water and menus.

While Courtney normally took a while to figure out what she wanted, her order here was always an easy decision. She just had to remember to put in a second order of crawfish poutine for Lucas on her way out.

"So tell me about Bob," Courtney said. "What's his story? You said he's a rescue?"

"Yeah. His last family didn't research the breed enough, I guess. Or thought they'd be able to train him out of his less-desirable habits and weren't up to the task. Happens to a lot of Sennies."

"Sennies?"

"Senegal parrots. I was fascinated with them when I was a kid. Nicole and I used to look up pictures of them all the time. I'd check out bird and parrot books from the library, and the Senegal parrots were always my favorite. I figured they'd make the best choice for an apartment someday."

So this wasn't some whim she'd jumped on.

Huh. Maybe Courtney had misjudged her. On this, at least.

"Sounds like he landed with someone who under-stands him this time. What was it they couldn't deal with? Noise?"

"Sennies have a rep for being a one-person bird. Or at least one type."

"One type?"

"He apparently hates men. And isn't afraid to show them just how much he hates them."

Courtney dropped her head and let a chuckle roll through her shoulders. She recovered from her giggle and said, "I'm guessing that might be a cramp in your dating style in the future, though."

It was none of her business. Not to mention something she didn't want to hear the details of.

But some curious piece of her wanted to know if that would be a problem. From what she'd heard, Vanessa had dated men and women in the past, but Courtney had only ever seen her in relationships with men.

It shouldn't matter. She shouldn't have even asked the question. Because this was still a line she wasn't prepared to cross. No matter how much Vanessa seemed to have changed.

"If it keeps Garett away," Vanessa said, "all the better."

Courtney wanted to press for details and ask if he'd been bothering Vanessa, but she wasn't sure how much to push. Vanessa had never wanted to talk about relationships in the past. More out of indifference, it seemed, but maybe that indifference was a mask, sort of like a performance game face.

"Has he been bugging you?" Courtney asked. "Other than when we saw him at the coffee shop?"

Vanessa shook her head. "He came by once, a few weeks ago, to get some of his stuff." She shifted uncomfortably. "Nothing happened. I'd just rather not talk about it."

"Do you miss playing with them?"

The look in Vanessa's eyes made Courtney wish

she could take those words back. But she couldn't unask the question.

"Never mind," Courtney said. "It's none of my business."

"No, it's fine. I liked playing with them. I like playing with just about anyone. And I can't lie, I did enjoy some of those bigger shows we did. But they weren't worth it. I don't miss them."

Courtney wasn't sure she understood. Of course, to her, bigger wasn't always better. The experience and the group dynamics were more important to Courtney than the size of a crowd. But she'd always had the impression that Vanessa was chasing bigger and better.

Had she misjudged Vanessa's values? Or was that something else that had changed?

"Sorry, I have to ask." Courtney couldn't miss this opportunity for clarification. To put her heart at ease or put Vanessa out of her mind. "I thought that was what you wanted. The big stage and all of that."

"It was," Vanessa said. "It still is."

"Is it because it wasn't big *enough*?"

She wasn't sure she wanted this answer. Nothing would ever be big enough for Vanessa. That idea was really what was eating at Courtney. It's what held her back from testing the waters here. From seeing if there was *something* else between them or if this was all in her head.

The idea that Vanessa would never be satisfied—with one band or one person—was the ultimate question. And while it was none of Courtney's business, she needed the answer. Or at least the best answer Vanessa could give her right now, even if she didn't know for sure.

"Yes and No. Of course, I still want to play huge gigs and have legions of fans. But not with people who lied to me."

That Courtney could understand. She remembered Vanessa telling her all of their big plans. From what she understood, they followed through on some of them. They went on tour, but it was a small regional one. They made a new album with Vanessa as lead guitar, but they didn't allow her any creative input on songs or set lists or which gigs they took like they'd promised. That disappointment would be hard to overcome.

"It wasn't just the breakup?" Courtney asked. "With Garrett?"

That was the other nagging question that made her sick to her stomach.

What if she took a chance here, and it didn't work out? What if Vanessa bailed again? What if the band fell apart again? Courtney couldn't handle that guilt.

Vanessa shook her head. "No. But it was easier to let everyone think that."

The server dropped off their food, and Courtney placed a to-go order for Lucas. When the server left, Courtney said, "I'm sorry. About both."

Courtney wasn't sorry about the failed relationship

or that the band hadn't worked out. Not just because it had worked out in Danger Dames' favor, but because they didn't seem like the best situation for Vanessa. She was just sorry Vanessa got hurt.

Vanessa shrugged. "The breakup sucked, and I sure as hell didn't want to see Garrett anymore. But I could have gotten over it. It wasn't like I was that into him anyway, and I knew who he was. It was just more lies on top of the manipulation that was already there. I couldn't stick around for more of the same."

"That makes sense."

"And honestly, I missed the whole team feeling," Vanessa said. "I don't mind doing random other gigs here and there, sitting in as more of a freelance thing. But if I'm going to be with a group, I want to feel that it's a real group effort. Like with us."

Courtney's eyes flicked up.

"With the band, I mean."

Courtney wanted to believe that look in Vanessa's eyes. The one that told her that *with us* meant more than just with the band. The one that hinted at her true feelings. Feelings that matched what Courtney was on the verge of finally admitting to herself.

But none of this convinced her that Vanessa's eternal dissatisfaction wasn't a real thing. That she'd changed.

Sure, she got a bird, but it remained to be seen if she'd follow through and take care of it. It was a huge commitment. And a long-term one, at that.

Time.

Courtney needed time to see if Vanessa could stick with her commitments. To let Vanessa prove herself and her intentions.

But her heart didn't want to wait.

It also didn't want to get stomped on.

Courtney dove into her meal, stabbing a shoestring fry and a crawfish tail and dragging them through the andouille gravy and cheese. She had to pause mid-chew as her taste buds exploded with the richness of the gravy along with the crisp, salty fries and spicy crawfish. It was just as good as she remembered. She and Lucas hadn't eaten here in a while, since it was a little pricey and they reserved it for special occasions only.

This felt like a special occasion.

"I have another question," Courtney said. "It's been bugging me since you brought it up, and I'm still curious."

Vanessa bit her lip, then said, "Shoot."

"Where did you get that bird from? I didn't realize there were bird rescue groups around here."

Vanessa's shoulders relaxed, and a grin stretched across her face. She was clearly grateful to steer out of that tough conversation. "Westbank Animal Warriors. The adoption coordinator said they don't normally take them in, but there wasn't any other rescue for this guy."

The piece of information Courtney had wondered

about clicked into place. "Wait a second. Who did you meet with?"

"Her name is Molly. I don't remember her last name."

Courtney laughed. "That's Jo's girlfriend."

The wheels behind Vanessa's eyes turned until it clicked for her, too. "Oh! I had no idea."

"Jo visited my booth last month when she brought up the festival, and we chatted a bit. It sounds like they're really happy together."

Vanessa smiled, but her delight over the other couple's happiness turned serious. She reached across the table to place her hand over Courtney's.

The warmth of Vanessa's palm on Courtney's skin sent heat radiating up her arm. Her breath hitched in her chest as she felt her cheeks flush. She hoped it wasn't visible.

But part of her hoped it was.

Part of her wanted Vanessa to know what effect her touch had.

"Thanks for helping me today," Vanessa said with a small, hesitant smile. A smile that hid so much hope behind it. A smile that made Courtney want to reach across the table and place her own mouth over it.

Shit. Get your act together.

"It wasn't a big deal," Courtney said. "But thanks for the food."

"It is a big deal." Vanessa bit her lip. "It's a big deal that you're giving me a chance."

A chance for what?

Courtney remained silent, frozen and speechless with that hand on hers. Afraid of what else might fall out of her mouth if she opened it again.

So she just nodded instead.

22

VANESSA

It took every ounce of control Vanessa had to not reach out and hold Courtney's hand while they walked together down the sidewalk. She'd never felt the urge for any kind of domestic bliss. Now all she wanted was an unending string of these quiet little moments with Courtney.

They'd talked about food and restaurants, Lucas and his therapy and school, art markets and online business, and how much Courtney had enjoyed teaching that resin class. All the fascinating tidbits of Courtney's life that Vanessa had been missing out on.

People who didn't know any better might think that Vanessa had the more interesting life over the last few years. And... maybe. But Courtney's life sounded more satisfying. Vanessa would never have believed it, but she wanted some of that comfort now.

"I guess I should head back," Courtney said as they

stopped in front of her car, a house down the street from Vanessa's place. She raised the plastic bag in her hand. "Lucas will start bombing my phone, looking for his food soon."

Vanessa's brain scrambled for some way to extend their time together. She considered promising the food would heat well, but that would be a lie. The French fries were already losing their crispness as they spoke, even though Simeon's did a good job of packing all the ingredients separately so the whole mess didn't get soggy.

She realized she was staring at Courtney's mouth while she tried to make up an excuse to have her stay a little longer. She couldn't help it. How had she never noticed before just how *kissable* those lips were?

Her phone dinged in her back pocket, but Vanessa ignored it. With every ounce of self-control being spent on *not* kissing Courtney, she didn't have any energy left for a text.

"Thanks so much for helping with Bob," Vanessa said. "I don't know how I would have gotten him inside without you."

"Of course," Courtney said, looking a little confused by Vanessa's gratitude. "I wouldn't turn my back on you when you need help."

"Yeah, but I know you're still upset with me."

Courtney frowned. "That's the thing, though. If you'd just talked to us beforehand, told us about it and about how you needed to give fame or whatever a shot, I would have understood."

Vanessa raised her brow at that. There was no amount of talking that would have made her exit okay. Which was partly why she hadn't bothered.

"Fine," Courtney conceded. "I would have still been upset. But if you'd explained that you needed to do that... it just... it would have made a difference."

That searing pain of guilt bore through her gut again. She should have trusted Courtney and the rest of them to have her back. She should have respected them enough to have that conversation and to help make sure they were covered in her absence. A transition or something.

"But I just bailed," she said. "And left you to deal with the fallout. That was on me. I get it. And I'm so, so sorry for that. I guess I was afraid."

Courtney looked confused again. "Afraid of what?"

"Your initial reaction," she said. "Even if you would eventually be okay, I didn't want to drag out my exit. I don't know if you know this, but you can be... intense."

She held her breath, hoping they were far enough into this apology tour for this level of honesty.

Courtney's eyes narrowed into a glare, but a tiny smirk made its way onto her mouth a second later.

"I don't know what you're talking about." She pulled out her phone and waved it in the air. "Better tell Lucas I'm on my way." She typed a quick text and sent it. "Pretty sure he's still got a crush on you."

"Well, tell him his sister already has my heart."

Oh.

Fuck.

Courtney stared back at her, that kissable mouth slightly open and jaw slack with shock.

Fuck, fuck, fuck.

Damn brain couldn't hold on and keep things under control for two more minutes.

"Forget I said that."

Courtney blinked at her, still staring. But Vanessa couldn't read her expression, and it was fucking killing her.

Finally, Courtney spoke. "I don't think I can."

"I know, I know," Vanessa said. "I know all the reasons. I get it. Let's just pretend I didn't say anything."

"No," Courtney said. Then, to Vanessa's complete shock, she reached out and took her hand as she said, "I meant I don't think I can forget you said that. I don't want to forget it."

Vanessa stared at their hands, now linked. When she looked up, she realized Courtney was waiting for a response. But for once, Vanessa was out of words. Out of action. Out of everything that made sense.

Courtney pulled back. "Unless I'm misreading things?"

"No," Vanessa blurted. "No. Not at all. I just... I

don't know. I get the impression you've got more reservations than I've got answers for."

"Yeah. My brain's not all in. Not yet." She held up the bag in her free hand. "And I'm worried about him."

"What does Lucas have to do with this?"

"Everything." Courtney looked dismayed. Like she didn't get why Vanessa couldn't understand something so simple and obvious. "I can't be another person who bails on him."

"I would never ask you to," Vanessa said. "I don't get it. He still has you, no matter what. And he's not a little kid anymore."

"No, but he still needs me."

Courtney's tone was growing defensive, so Vanessa rolled back the conversation a bit.

"Okay, sure. He'll always need his big sister," Vanessa said. "And you'll always be there for him."

"But I wasn't the other night."

It pained Vanessa to see her like this. She understood Courtney's protective instinct. Understood her past and the damage their mother had done. But Vanessa couldn't sit by and watch this play out without saying something.

"You *were* there when he called. You can't stay at home or hover over him forever. You have to live your life, too."

"Not at the expense of not being there for him," Courtney said.

"I would never ask you to do that. Part of what

makes you so amazing is your caring and loyalty. I would never ask you to put that aside. I would never ask you to not be you."

Courtney's eyes filled with tears as she stepped closer, now taking both of Vanessa's hands down by her thighs, the takeout bag dangling from her fingers and bumping against Vanessa's leg. Courtney held her gaze firm and managed a shattered, "Thank you."

Vanessa squeezed her hands in return and closed the space between them.

What was she doing?

Wait... what was Courtney doing?

Before Vanessa's brain stumbled through processing the situation, Courtney leaned in and connected her mouth with Vanessa's.

Vanessa had been holding back for over an hour, fighting the urge to meet that mouth with her own, and now it was happening.

She was *kissing Courtney*.

And it wasn't just any kiss. Courtney's lips still tasted of Creole spices, and her hand was warm as she brought it up to hold the side of Vanessa's face.

She was *kissing Courtney*.

Her brain was stuck in a loop, but the rest of her body took over, hungry for more. Eager to enjoy this moment and make it last.

Because surely this would all vanish soon.

Right?

It felt real enough. The kiss was warm and had a

gentle urgency, like Courtney had been holding back, just like Vanessa had been holding back. Like they'd both been wanting the same thing this whole time.

Courtney released Vanessa's hand and held up the bag. "I'd better get this back to Lucas. He could use the fuel for that paper he needs to finish."

"Maybe we can hang out tomorrow?" Vanessa had never heard her own voice sound so small or hesitant before. Never with a romantic partner. Or even a potential one. She was always the person in control.

Okay, that wasn't entirely true.

She'd heard that voice before. When she'd asked her parents to come to one of her first shows. She'd been a teenager, barely an adult. The band she was with was playing at a restaurant, so she thought she could convince her parents to come watch her play since it wasn't at a grimy little bar.

They'd laughed and asked if she was getting paid in chips and salsa.

They didn't show up.

"Maybe. I don't have an arts market this weekend. I just have to pack up some orders to take to the post office on Monday."

"Maybe I could come over while you do that? Or after."

Courtney smiled. "That sounds nice. I'll text you?"

"Yeah. Let me know when's a good time." Vanessa gave her another small kiss and used up every ounce of willpower she had to step back and release her grip on

Courtney's hand. "Tell Lucas I said hi. Thanks again for the help."

"Thanks for dinner." Courtney got behind the wheel and stuck her head out the window. "Tell Bob I said to enjoy his first night in his new place!"

Once Courtney's car disappeared down the street, Vanessa checked the text she'd gotten a few minutes before and ignored. The name attached to it made her want to throw her phone down a drain. Or maybe let Bob chew on it. But her eyes eventually scanned past the name to the message.

Shit.

She was hoping it was just something obnoxious. Something she could ignore. Or send a dismissive reply at the very least.

Unfortunately, she needed to deal with this.

To consider this.

She gnawed on the side of her thumb while she reread the text.

The Kings of Canal's new guitarist, her replacement, would be out of town. They needed a sub for the next week. A big Halloween party and a few smaller midweek gigs. Since Vanessa knew all the tunes, she was their first obvious choice.

Being the obvious choice, however, didn't make it a simple choice for her.

On the surface, it was a straightforward decision. She could take any of the gigs that didn't interfere with nights she was booked, which was just the bi-weekly gig with Danger Dames so far.

As much as she meant every word to Courtney about how she didn't want to play with those people anymore, she couldn't deny that she could use the extra easy money. She'd overestimated how far her barista paychecks would stretch, and their current gigs weren't enough to pay her bills. Not with the arrangement she'd made with Nicole.

No, she wouldn't regret that decision.

Still, she had bird food and other supplies to buy.

It would have helped if she'd thought through or budgeted some of this stuff, but it was too late to second-guess any of that now.

She had to take the offer.

This was just a temporary thing that wouldn't interfere with the band going forward, but she doubted Courtney would see it that way. This choice would bring up old wounds and feel like another betrayal. Or Courtney would see it as a stepping stone to a repeat betrayal.

Vanessa texted back that she needed the night to think it over. What she really needed was a plan to make sure Courtney knew without a doubt that Vanessa was committed to her and to the Dames before she dropped this news.

23

COURTNEY

"Oh, come on! I know I hit him!"

The shout, followed by a flurry of video game explosions, startled Courtney enough to put a long ink tail at the end of that line of lyrics. She was almost finished a song she'd been dabbling with for the last couple of weeks. Lyrics she'd started working on years ago, but never quite had a handle on.

"Ha! Got him!" Vanessa beamed with pride, propped against the couch on the floor near Courtney's feet.

Lucas put his controller down and gave her a fist bump. "Nice shot."

Vanessa peered over Courtney's leg and saw the scribble on the side of the page. "Oh, shit. Sorry."

"It's fine," Courtney said. "I'll type it all up later, anyway. These are just my notes."

The pretty journal with the fairy garden on the

cover had been with Courtney since she was a teenager. She only wrote songs in it. A hobby she didn't engage in very often. Only when she felt inspired by something. She'd finished up two over the past week. Ever since she'd helped Vanessa get that bird in her apartment. More importantly, ever since that kiss. The first, but definitely not the last.

Maybe Vanessa was becoming her muse.

Not that Courtney believed in muses. She believed in hard work and showing up, but she did like being inspired. Writing songs wasn't her job, so she saved it for a special activity. She pulled it out only when she really wanted to do it. Lately, there were a lot of things she wanted to do that she'd pushed aside for too many years.

Vanessa hobbled to her knees and scooted close to Courtney, resting her arms on Courtney's leggings and looking up with those big, dark eyes of hers as a sly grin made its way to her face. "Can I read them?"

"Not yet." Courtney planted a quick kiss on Vanessa's mouth, then lingered inches away. "I just showed you that other one a couple of days ago."

"I know, but I want to see this one, too. I'm greedy for your words, and I don't care if you know that."

"Patience."

"Do I need to leave or are we gonna finish this level?" Lucas waved his controller in the air. "I've got class in a little while."

"I'm coming, I'm coming." Vanessa spun around

and plopped back down on the floor. "I will not be responsible for making you late. Your sister would kill me deader than this guy I'm about to eradicate."

"I'm not killing anyone," Courtney said. "But I do have to drop Lucas off at his class."

"I'll be out of your hair soon. Unless you want me to drop him off for you so you can get some work done?"

Courtney had caught up on her online orders the day before and had been pushing to make more stock for the upcoming fall and holiday markets. She still had lots to make and do in the months ahead, and her insomnia had her moving slower during her days than she'd like, but she'd planned to take today off to spend it with Vanessa while she wasn't scheduled at the coffee shop. Since the band had decided things were in good enough shape to skip tonight's rehearsal and just do the gig tomorrow night, Courtney had all day and night to spend with Vanessa.

This was the first sizable chunk of time they'd carved out together since they'd made the leap to give this relationship thing a shot. But Courtney wasn't ready to make a big announcement about it to the band, so they planned to hold off on public dates for a while. Unfortunately, that limited their options. Not that Courtney minded staying in with Vanessa, but she wanted to experience the city with her. They'd been friends for a while, but it still felt like they had so much to catch up on. Plus three years of lost time.

Nope. She wasn't thinking about that. At least not today.

"I'm all yours," Courtney said. "Do you need to feed Bob or anything?"

"Not until later. All yours today, too."

An enormous explosion hit the screen again, and Lucas tossed his controller to the side. "I don't want to be a witness to all this togetherness. I'm going to get ready while you two decide which of you is dropping me off."

Vanessa swiveled around and tilted her head at Courtney like an adorable puppy. "We can both go?"

"Perfect."

Asking about Bob had put an idea in her brain. An even more perfect idea than just dropping off Lucas at his class. And one that wouldn't out their relationship to anyone in the band and would also give them the entire afternoon together.

"What's that look for?"

Courtney grinned. "I've got an idea."

"Oh yeah? Does it involve me?"

"Absolutely."

"Do tell," Vanessa said with interest.

Courtney leaned forward to take Vanessa's face in both hands and kiss her, playfully at first, but she couldn't help the passion that overtook it.

Remembering she still had to bring her brother to class, Courtney pulled away and smiled.

"It's a surprise."

24

VANESSA

The car came to a stop, but Vanessa didn't know where they were. Courtney had made her keep her eyes closed the entire drive.

"Okay," Courtney said. "You can open them now."

Vanessa blinked against the sunlight streaming into Courtney's windshield and squinted across the massive parking lot as she struggled to figure out where they were. Her direction sense was shit, so she'd lost track of their path after only three or four turns out of Courtney's neighborhood. Eventually, her focus narrowed on the center of the wide entrance up ahead, where a familiar sign was perched. Audubon Zoo.

"You brought me on a zoo date?"

Courtney's expression was a bizarre mix of pride, excitement, and sheer terror. No doubt worried she'd made a horrible mistake or something equally ridiculous. She nodded in response.

"This is the *best*." Vanessa reached over the gearshift to grab Courtney's face and kiss her. Hard. Then she continued to hold her as she looked into her hazel eyes and said, "Thank you."

Courtney exhaled. "I was hoping you'd like it." She glanced at the entrance, then back at Vanessa. "And I figured we'd be pretty safe not running into anyone we know here."

That stung more than Vanessa would have liked, but she realized it wasn't because Courtney was embarrassed to be seen with her. Courtney needed time to settle into their relationship before inviting anyone else in on the secret.

The upside was Vanessa had Courtney all to herself, without having to face questions about her past or history repeating. The two of them could just... be. Together.

Vanessa clapped her hands and spun around for the door handle. "Let's go, let's go, let's go!"

Courtney's laughter as she locked the car was pure magic.

Vanessa swore to make Courtney laugh, that beautiful carefree sound, as often as possible. Today and every day she was lucky enough to have the opportunity.

———

THE AVIARY WAS a straight shot from the entrance, just past the carousel. Vanessa promised they'd swing back for the exhibits they skipped on the way to the aviary, but Courtney said not to worry about it.

Even though it was a gorgeous, sunny day in the mid-sixties, the zoo wasn't crowded. Every post and walkway was decorated for Halloween, but most of the local traffic came on the weekends. Weekdays were mostly for field trips and preschoolers, who were all back at school or at home for nap times by now. And October wasn't a popular tourist time. Although it should be. In Vanessa's mind, October was the best month of the year in New Orleans weather-wise, not counting the hurricanes. Thankfully, the Gulf had been quiet so far. It seemed it was Florida's turn for activity this time around.

"Look how pretty," Courtney said once they were inside the free-flight aviary. She pointed at a beautiful indigo-colored bird with stunning blue and green wings sitting on a palm near the entrance. "He's gorgeous. Do you know what kind that is?"

"A pigeon. A Nicobar, I think." It had been a long time since Vanessa had visited the zoo, and even longer since she'd read up on bird species. That obsession had taken a backseat to her music for the last decade.

They wandered over the walkway with Courtney cooing about some birds she'd never seen before and quizzing Vanessa on them. As much fun as it was to be back in here, it was even more fun to see it all through

Courtney's eyes. And it was so good seeing Courtney relaxed and enjoying herself. She deserved this carefree break, even if she hadn't suggested it for herself.

"Do you hear that?"

Courtney turned her head, craning her ear one way, then another. "That sweet little song?"

"Yes, that." Vanessa scanned the canopy until she found him and pointed at the bright golden weaver. "There. Building a nest."

"Oh, he's so cute!" Courtney turned to Vanessa and examined her curiously. "What is it about birds that you love so much? I mean, they're cute, but I've never met anyone who loves them like you do."

Vanessa shrugged. "Always have. I don't know. They just... do their thing. They're bright and colorful and no one gives them shit for singing or drawing attention to themselves. They're loud and proud and beloved for it."

Her mom would constantly tell her to be quiet, and she never cared about Vanessa's music or anything else she was into. Ever. Vanessa had never put that together with how much she'd wanted to be one of those birds. Even in cages, they were still free to be themselves.

Courtney slipped her arm around Vanessa's and leaned in to kiss her cheek. "I love your version of loud and proud."

Vanessa smiled at her and kissed her nose. "And I could listen to you sing all day, too."

Courtney blushed. "You want to hang out here

longer? Or are you ready to check out some other stuff? I want to see if they have any tarantulas to report back to Sage on."

"Yeah, we can head that way. I think there's one up ahead. If they haven't moved things around since I was last here."

They made their way out of the aviary and headed to the next area. They passed through an archway decorated with ghosts and black cats.

"Oh, that reminds me," Courtney said. "Do you want to come with me to a Halloween party at Sage and Brooke's place next weekend?"

Vanessa's stomach clenched with dread. She'd wanted to tell Courtney today about the gigs, figuring it would be better to get it over with. Rip off the bandage. But she didn't want to ruin this. For herself, but also for Courtney. It was so good to see her relaxing and having a a great time. Vanessa didn't want to ruin that.

"I thought we weren't going public yet," she said, hoping the reminder would get her out of this without having to kill the mood of the day.

"It's just a small thing, and maybe it could be a trial run to be together around people before we tell the band?"

Dammit.

She wished she could be excited about Courtney wanting to tell people about their relationship, but there was too much else to worry about.

"I wish I could, but I picked up a shift. Covering for someone that night."

There. That wasn't a lie. She just wouldn't correct Courtney if she assumed Vanessa meant covering for someone at the cafe.

Vanessa hated the disappointment on Courtney's face. A reminder that she would hate even more how disappointed Courtney would be once she found out the truth.

But Vanessa would come clean next week about it all and they'd figure it out. For now, Courtney needed this. They both did.

"Maybe we can do something else that weekend."

"Yeah, for sure." Vanessa squeezed Courtney's hand and pulled her along. "Come on. Let's go find a spider."

25

COURTNEY

COURTNEY TOOK A SIP FROM THE TRAVEL MUG she'd brought with her. The honey coated her throat while she savored the hibiscus and green tea blend.

Vanessa had bought a bag of the cafe tea for Courtney so she could make her own before gigs and rehearsals. It was the most thoughtful thing Courtney could remember anyone doing for her.

"Okay, what gives?" Nicole stood in front of her, hands on her hips. "You got good news or what?"

"No. Why?"

"Because I haven't seen you this happy in like... ever," Nicole said. "No, I lie. Maybe Lucas's graduation."

That had been a a joyful day. It had been hell getting Lucas over that finish line, but he'd done it. And the pride in his eyes and smile when he walked across that stage had been worth all the stress and long nights helping him write papers and cram for finals to make sure he passed his classes. The band had been with her too, all cheering for Lucas right along with her.

The whole band except one person.

But that person was making up for lost time now, and the past week had been pretty great. Pretty great was an understatement, actually. Courtney couldn't remember the last time she'd felt so relaxed. Even if they hadn't gone out much together, except for that zoo trip. She'd been happy to just *be*. At her own place listening to Lucas and Vanessa laughing and playing video games while she wrote or made new items for her shop. Or at Vanessa's apartment, their legs tangled on the couch while Bob hung out with them, whistling and showing off his vocabulary of sounds and a few short phrases.

"Just in a good mood, I guess." Her gaze was pulled to the door as Vanessa walked in with her guitar bag slung over one shoulder.

Nicole followed Courtney's line of sight. "Liar."

Panic gripped Courtney as she realized Nicole was on to them. They weren't keeping their relationship a secret, not really, but Courtney wasn't ready to share it with the group. It was easier to keep things low-key and slow-paced if they didn't have to talk about it yet.

Okay, maybe it was also because this way she didn't have to face that it was real.

Whatever the reason, they were keeping things quiet.

Maybe not quiet enough, though.

"What do you think I'm lying about?"

"Listen," Nicole said, her voice a firm but hushed tone. "I know you both long before today. And you're both grown-ass adults who can do what you want. Honestly? I'm happy as hell for both of you. If you can both get out of your own damn way, I think you'd make each other really happy."

Courtney's gaze flicked again to Vanessa, who gave a small smile as she put her gear down in her spot.

How had Nicole put this together on basically nothing?

"I don't know what—"

"Stop." Nicole put a hand up to halt the denial. "Just be happy for once, Court."

Courtney let out a stream of air, releasing all of her anxieties with it. All of her hesitations. Then, she said the truest thing she'd said in a long time. "I am happy. I want this to work. More than I've let myself want anything in a long time. It's just... I'm scared. If it doesn't work, I want things to still be ok. For all of us."

"Then let things be ok," Nicole said. "We're *all* adults here. We can all deal with this. I promise. Let us."

She knew she had to let people be themselves and take care of their own stuff. Give them a chance to do the right things and pick things up when they fell apart. Vanessa. Her brother. The rest of the band. She had to stop trying to make things okay for everyone else and let them handle matters, too.

"You're right. It's just... I don't know. I just don't know if we can make this work."

Nicole glanced at Vanessa. "I know she's a lot. But you are too. Just be a lot together."

Courtney couldn't say anything else. Her words were all choked in her throat.

"Better finish getting set up so we can get on with this." Nicole turned and walked back to her area.

She was right. About both topics, but especially about needing to set up. They needed to get rehearsal rolling. They had a lot of tunes to run through and only one rehearsal left before the festival in three weeks. Not to mention the new song.

Courtney had stayed up all night after their trip to the zoo finishing it. She wasn't sleeping anyway, might as well make use of the awake time and do something productive. Especially while her heart was light, and she had all kinds of creative juices flowing again. It had been so long since she'd been in a groove like that. She didn't realize how much she'd missed writing songs. Maybe even more than she'd missed singing and performing.

"Do we want to focus on the new song today?" Courtney asked. "We can schedule another rehearsal to run through everything else later. Since we don't have a whole lot of time to get this in shape before the festival."

Nicole grabbed her phone to check out her calendar. "How about next Thursday? I know we've been skipping rehearsal on Friday gig weeks, but we could do both next week. Even do a trial run of the new song at the bar."

"As long as we're done in time for me to pick up Lucas from work, I'm good any evening."

Emily and Libby chimed in that any Thursday was fine with them as well.

"I can't," Vanessa said with a forced hesitance, like she had to push out each of those words.

Courtney eyed her curiously. They'd had no problems getting together in the evenings over the last few days. Vanessa didn't have any other commitments besides the coffee shop and that bird, as far as Courtney knew. "I thought you just worked days, except this weekend for Halloween."

"I do. At the cafe." Vanessa shifted back and forth. Courtney recognized her itch to pace, like she always did when she was nervous about something. "I picked up some sub gigs next week."

The sentence was a direct punch to Courtney's gut. She was nauseated from the impact, and her pulse kicked up. It was happening all over again. And after less than two months.

"You're still on for all of our gigs though, right?" Emily asked in a hopeful voice.

"Yeah," Vanessa said, her eyes not leaving Courtney. "I'm still in for everything. I just don't have free evenings to add anything."

"So we're *not* your priority after all." Courtney's voice was dripping with pain and anger.

"Yes, you are. I'm not sitting in on the dates I already have booked with you. And this is only for one week."

"We'll just have to get everything in then," Nicole said. "Maybe we can stay a little later today."

"Can't." Courtney cleared her throat, trying to clear out the shakiness from it. She didn't want to let on to the rest of the band that this was rattling her. Although her hands were already shaking at her sides. "I have to pick up Lucas."

Libby asked, "Can you drop him off and come back real quick?"

Courtney breathed through the all too familiar gut-punch. One fierce, hurt-fueled breath after another. She took each breath through her nose, afraid of what words might tumble out if she opened her mouth.

But they needed an answer.

"I guess."

The matter was settled.

Nicole nodded and said, "Then let's do that and get started."

26

VANESSA

THE SKIN AROUND VANESSA'S THUMB WAS A chewed-up mess. She'd been avoiding her nails because it was harder to keep clean under there and more important not to get Bob's germs in her mouth. But she'd shifted her noshing to just one thumb. It didn't affect her playing, and she kept it as clean as possible, wearing a bandage when it got too raw.

While the past week had been wonderful, her time spent with Courtney hadn't erased her unease about her upcoming week of playing with Kings of Canal. Her feelings about it only being temporary hadn't changed, but her guilt about not telling Courtney had only grown.

Vanessa should have told her before this. But it was too late for that now.

Courtney had rushed out during their break to pick up Lucas without a glance Vanessa's way. Vanessa had known better than to talk to her then. Never stand in the way of Courtney taking care of her brother. Not even for a second.

Vanessa would catch her when she came back. Or after rehearsal.

She needed to plead her case. Again. She was always pleading her case with Courtney. Was she setting herself up for an entire relationship revolving around pleading her case to this woman?

Nicole dragged a stool over to sit beside Vanessa. In a low voice, she said, "I told you to take things slow."

"I was taking things slow," Vanessa argued. When Nicole gave her a look, Vanessa added, "Fine. I took things slow for me. Maybe it wasn't slow enough for Court. But maybe I can't go that fucking slow, okay?"

"Hey, it's not my shit on the line here. Don't come at me with that."

"Sorry." And she was. She was sorry she'd snapped at Nicole. Sorry she'd had to take those gigs she didn't even want. Sorry she'd hurt Courtney. Again.

"You need to tell her."

"Tell her what?"

"Why you took the gigs," Nicole said. "I know you need the money."

"I'm not telling her that." That was the last thing Vanessa wanted to do. If she was going to ease things with Courtney, she'd have to do it some other way. "And don't you say anything either."

"I won't. Not if you don't want me to. But you should."

Vanessa scoffed. "Who was I kidding? This was doomed from the start. Her instinct is probably right about me, anyway."

"That you're a self-pitying mess?"

"That I'll never stick with anything."

"You're sticking with us," Nicole said. "Didn't you say you turned down some of the gigs they offered?"

"Right. This time. What about next time? What about when something bigger comes along?"

What about if some*one* else comes along?

Vanessa had to consider whether she really had commitment in her bones. Commitment to anything. She'd never thought so before, but being with Courtney had made her wonder. Maybe she just hadn't found anything she wanted to commit to until now. Courtney and this band were definitely worth that commitment.

Then again, maybe she was only fooling herself.

"You're looking for an easy out 'cause you're scared right now."

"So what am I supposed to do? Just not be scared? How does that work?"

"You are one of the most fearless people I have ever known," Nicole said. "Even when I have seen you afraid, you've barreled right through it. Just do that."

Vanessa laughed. *Just do that.* It sounded so fucking simple.

"It doesn't matter," she said. "Court will never trust me. I tried to do the right thing this time. Then I fumbled a little, and look at how she reacted. I can't promise to never fuck up at all. She'll always be waiting for it."

Nicole stood and dragged the stool back to where she'd found it. "Just talk to her. Be honest. Work it out."

Nicole went outside, leaving Vanessa alone in her corner while Emily and Libby talked among themselves and avoided her.

COURTNEY WAS ONLY GONE twenty-five minutes, and the band jumped right back into the next song the second her feet entered the room. An hour and a half later, they wrapped up rehearsal, and Vanessa hurried outside with her guitar bag slung over one shoulder to wait beside Courtney's car.

As expected, Courtney didn't look pleased to find her there.

"Can we talk for a second?"

Courtney scowled. "Not sure what there is to talk about."

"I want to talk about why you're pissed off," Vanessa said. "And what I can do to ease whatever you're worried about."

"I'm not *worried* about anything. I'm hurt. And

I'm... I'm just disappointed, is all. Even though I knew better."

"Hold up." Vanessa stood up a little straighter while Courtney threw her purse into the car. "Knew better than what? What exactly did I do that was so horrible this time?"

Courtney froze, then turned to face Vanessa. She stared at her a good long while before speaking. "You picked them. Again."

"I didn't pick anyone, dammit. I took some gigs because they pay well."

Courtney narrowed her eyes in challenge. "I thought you said you never wanted to play with them again."

"I don't. This is a one-week thing. And no, I'm not looking forward to it, but I could use the money."

"Because you adopted a bird you couldn't pay for."

Vanessa sighed and looked at the stars shining down on them from a clear night sky. "Fine. I didn't plan ahead well enough. But I'm fixing it."

"What happens the next time you can't pay for something you impulse buy like that bird? How long before you bail on us again for a better opportunity? How long before you pick some other band again?"

Vanessa pulled her gaze from the sky and looked into Courtney's hazel eyes. She found exactly what she expected to see in them. Distrust. Pain. Anger. It didn't matter how many times she apologized or how many ways she tried to explain that she was committed to them now. It was all pointless.

"You're never going to forgive me for that, are you?"

Courtney just stared back at her. It was clear that even if she wanted to, Courtney didn't know how to forgive her, much less how to trust her. Vanessa was beginning to doubt if Courtney could ever trust *anyone*.

Vanessa knew where that distrust came from. She knew enough to know how painful it had been for Courtney to have her mom walk out on them. How hard it was to take care of Lucas and manage all the responsibilities that came with that.

But Vanessa couldn't fix the past. And she couldn't stand to be another person in Courtney's life who continually let her down.

"Do we just admit this was a mistake or what?"

"Is that what you want?" Every word was ragged, as if it had been torn from Courtney's throat like a page from a notebook.

Vanessa wanted to scream, *No!* But she didn't know what other option they had. She couldn't make Courtney trust or forgive her. She thought time alone could do that. But after only a couple weeks, the smallest bump was putting them right back where they'd started. What good would more time do?

"I don't want to fight with you," she said. "And I don't want to lose the band."

Courtney pressed her lips together, seeming to come to the same conclusion. "Then we rewind the past couple of weeks. We go back to being bandmates only. I don't want to fight anymore, either."

Vanessa nodded, even though her insides were screaming at her to stop this before it was too late. "Okay then. Friends?"

Courtney thought for a moment, then said. "We'll see."

Vanessa moved aside so Courtney could get in the driver's seat. She stood in stunned silence and watched Courtney drive away, wondering how this all went so wrong so fast.

27

COURTNEY

A crisp wind cut across Courtney's face as it blasted through a side street Downtown. It was as if the weather knew the calendar had turned the page to November and decided to shift gears and cool down with it.

Courtney loved fall weather, and this front was pushing a tropical storm threat east of them. She kind of felt bad for the folks in Florida getting a late-season storm, but Louisiana had its fair share last year. It was someone else's turn. This system wasn't predicted to do much, so she didn't feel too guilty about wishing it elsewhere.

Now she could kick back and enjoy the shifting season, even if it was a brief respite. Warm weather was returning to the forecast next week, but at least the cold, windy days fit her current mood.

Her walk to the art gallery was a short one since

she'd lucked out finding a closer spot than last time. She took a sip of the tea she'd brought from home and winced at the bitterness of the green tea. She couldn't bring herself to make the stuff Vanessa had brought her, and the only other tea she had on hand paled in comparison. The bitter brew tasted like sadness.

Great, she was in a mood. And right before her last class, too.

Courtney had crossed the street long before she reached Crescent Cafe and kept her eyes on the sidewalk as she passed it. She wrestled with her brain to not relive that first day she'd seen Vanessa there or the conversation they'd had at that outside table.

She didn't even know if Vanessa was working right now, but she couldn't take the chance. Seeing her again at rehearsals and gigs would be awkward enough. She didn't also want to catch sight of each other through the giant coffee shop windows.

Maybe one day things would get easier. Maybe the memories of Vanessa and the hope Courtney had dared to hold would fade from her mind. Things would be back to the way they were before Vanessa left the band. When they were just bandmates and friends. Back when Courtney didn't feel like she was dying inside every time she saw Vanessa.

Sage was already in the little classroom when Courtney walked in. She was placing a handout at each seat around the tables.

"Hey there." Sage brightened even more when she

saw Courtney enter the room. "Feels like forever since I've seen you."

Courtney hadn't been avoiding her. Not exactly. But she hadn't been as chatty for the last several days. And she'd skipped out on their weekly trip to the post office together, claiming she didn't have any shop orders to mail. She wasn't ready to talk about any of what went down.

"Been a busy week."

"Uh-oh." Sage froze after placing the last paper on the far table as she stared across the room at Courtney. "What's wrong?"

Sage could always tell when something was wrong. Not just with Courtney, but with anyone.

"It's just band stuff."

That wasn't a lie. It did affect the band. That impact was part of the reason she'd been confident about ending things with Vanessa, even though her heart had screamed at her for a full twenty-four hours after their last conversation to *fix* this.

There was no fixing this. Only making sure this didn't also break the band. That had to be the priority right now.

But it wasn't *just* band stuff that was bothering her. And Sage wouldn't let her slide that easily.

Sage crossed the room and patted the nearest table, urging Courtney to sit with her. "Tell me. All of it."

"I need to set up." She'd shown up extra early, with plenty of time to prepare and relax before students arrived. But it also made a good excuse to keep moving and avoid baring her soul. Or at least the best excuse she could come up with.

"We have plenty of time," Sage said. "And you'll have more energy once you get whatever this is off your chest. So spill it."

Courtney contemplated how to tell Sage what had happened. Where to start. How to keep her emotions in check so she didn't end up in a puddle of tears right before class.

She decided there was no other way than straight through it.

"Vanessa and I broke up."

"Oh, no." Sage placed her hand over Courtney's on the table. "I'm so sorry. What happened? I thought things were off to a good start."

Courtney gave a quick recap of the whole mess of that rehearsal. Vanessa's announcement that she was playing with her old band and her ex despite insisting she wanted nothing to do with them again. How she hadn't even bothered to tell Courtney about it before announcing the fact at rehearsal in front of everyone else. And finally, their last conversation outside by Courtney's car.

"You haven't spoken to her since then?"

Courtney shook her head. "She's been playing with the other group all week, so I won't see her except for our gig in a couple of days."

Courtney wasn't ready to see Vanessa again so

soon. It had only been a week since their breakup. She needed more time away. Time to lick her wounds and get used to the idea that they had no future together.

This was why dating a bandmate was such a bad plan. There was no space or time to get over something like this. She'd known it was a terrible idea and had jumped in anyway.

"Oh, honey. I'm so sorry."

"It's better this way." It was the mantra Courtney had created for herself and repeated all week. "This would have ended, eventually. We weren't a good match. It's better to accept that fact now and keep the band intact before things go too far to come back from."

"It sounded like you were a good match to me."

Courtney laughed. "Did I not tell you about her at all?"

"A good match doesn't mean someone who's the same as you. What if your differences were what could make you perfect together?"

"I don't see how that would be possible here," Courtney said. "Vanessa will always do what Vanessa wants. Without thinking ahead. I can't do that. I've got responsibilities."

"But maybe that's why it would be great. You could smooth each other out a bit." Sage shook her head. "But that's not really the point, is it?"

"The point is, she chose them again. She lied about not wanting to play with them anymore, and she kept the fact that she was doing it from me."

Sage nodded. "And you were already struggling to trust her."

"Right." Courtney swallowed her hurt with a swig of bitter tea. "Chalking it up to a failed experiment."

"Is there any chance she had a good reason for not telling you? Or taking the jobs in the first place?"

Courtney shrugged. "I don't know if it matters."

She could have given Vanessa a better chance to explain herself. She could have had all of her questions answered with a phone call or text.

But she'd chosen not to.

She'd chosen the band and protecting herself.

Sage squeezed her hand. "I'm really sorry. I was rooting for you two."

"Thanks." Courtney stood and picked up her bag. "I should start setting up. I could use the distraction."

"That's fair." Sage grinned. "A round of equal parts celebratory and wallowing jalapeño margaritas? My treat?"

"Sounds perfect."

Courtney began taking supplies out of her bag, feeling a tad lighter in the warmth of Sage's caring.

She didn't need Vanessa or anyone else right now. Her life was full already. Full of responsibilities and family *and* friendship. She didn't need anything else.

If only her heart believed that.

28

VANESSA

THE AIR IN THE ALLEY WAS JARRINGLY COLD compared to the sweaty bar Vanessa had just exited. She stood only a few feet from a dumpster, but it still smelled better out there than inside.

She'd forgotten how awful these Kings of Canal gigs were. They were always in places that didn't give a fuck about capacity regulations and even less a fuck about clashes between locals with a chip on their shoulders and loud-mouthed tourists who wandered in from their short-term rentals trying to pretend they were anything but out of place and outnumbered.

When the most recent skirmish had broken out just after their last set, Vanessa decided to wait for her payment outside. She didn't want to talk to anyone in the band, and she sure as hell didn't want to share a post-performance round. Thankfully, this was her last gig with them. For this week and forever.

The weird thing was that this didn't feel much different from when she'd been a full member of the band. Only now she didn't care about that lack of connection. That wasn't what she was here for.

She wasn't playing with them for prestige or valida-tion anymore. All she wanted was to get paid, then go home to her bird and her bed. Alone.

The delivery door opened beside her, and Garrett stepped out into the alley. His smug grin made her want to vomit, but his appearance had one very impor-tant perk. The sooner he paid her, the sooner she could leave.

Vanessa pushed off from the wall and held out her hand. Garrett placed some folded cash in her palm but didn't release it.

"This doesn't have to be the last one, you know."

Vanessa narrowed her eyes. "I thought the new guy was just out of town. Did he get sick of you already?"

"I may have exaggerated his status with us. I've been hiring him on a temporary basis." Garrett shrugged. "Figured you'd be back eventually, so we didn't bring in an official replacement."

How could she not have seen this coming? Garrett was made of manipulation. He'd do anything to get what he wanted.

The only difference this time was she hadn't been looking out for it. She'd been so focused on taking responsibility for her own actions that she hadn't seen it coming.

She snatched her payment from his fingers. "You, of all people, should know how much I hate being lied to and manipulated. You thought *that* would win me over?"

"I figured I could lure you here, and the money would do the rest." Garrett nodded at the building behind him. "That and the applause. We both know you love an audience. You can't make yourself small with those people for long."

"Those people are my friends," she said with a fierceness she hadn't expected. "And they actually give a shit about me and know me better than to think lies and a stack of cash are enough to make me happy."

Was that true, though?

For most of the band, yes. They knew her better than that.

But did Courtney?

Vanessa tilted her head back and looked at the sky. Of course, Courtney didn't know that, because Vanessa hadn't shown her the truth. Not really. She hadn't trusted her with it. Not about taking these gigs or why she'd taken them in the first place. She'd withheld that information, telling herself she didn't want to upset Courtney.

She prided herself on being brave and living in the moment and going after what she wanted, but she was just scared.

Garrett and this whole band sucked because they were full of half-truths and bullshit. She'd left that behind for better, but she'd brought her own bullshit and dropped it right in Courtney's lap.

She'd really fucked this up. And it was her own damn fault for not being honest. For not trusting Courtney to handle the truth if Vanessa had been upfront about it all. For not being as brave as she claimed to be.

She snatched the envelope from Garrett's grip. "Do me a favor. Lose my number."

"We might need a sub again," he said to her back as she walked away.

Confident this was the last time she'd ever speak to him, Vanessa called out over her shoulder, "Find someone else."

———

THE FOLLOWING NIGHT, Vanessa was back on stage. This time, she was with Danger Dames for their biweekly show in the cozy little bar with the women who were the closest thing she had to family.

She'd long ago stopped talking to her blood relatives. Didn't even bother to rub it in their noses that she was an actual working musician, because that still wouldn't be good enough for them. But it was good enough for her. *This* was good enough for her.

Despite the tension between her and Courtney, the performance was, as always, a rewarding experience. Their energy and talent meshed perfectly on stage, and the crowd loved them. It felt satisfying to follow up last night's depressing gig with this one. A reminder that she wasn't missing out on anything. She had everything she could want right here with these people.

Well, almost everything.

Courtney wasn't antagonistic or even standoffish. She took part in conversations when she was included. She smiled and laughed. She was friendly, but still distant. Her wall was up. The wall that made it clear no one was getting in.

Vanessa was winding up her cables when she saw Courtney stop to say something to Emily, then head towards the front of the bar. She'd mentioned she didn't have to pick up Lucas tonight, so Vanessa had assumed she'd stick around for a group drink before they all headed out.

"Is she leaving?" Vanessa asked.

Emily frowned. It was obvious she was conflicted, but Vanessa wasn't sure if Emily was conflicted about revealing specific information or about getting involved at all.

Vanessa and Courtney hadn't revealed their relationship or breakup to the band, but the others had to know something was up.

"Yeah. She said she didn't feel great," Emily said. "What did you do?"

Vanessa bit her tongue, fighting the instinct to defend herself. To deny that she'd done anything wrong. To blame Courtney's stubbornness.

But she couldn't.

She was done deflecting and done not taking responsibility for her part in things. She might not own all the blame here, but she owned enough.

"Thanks. Can you watch my stuff a sec?" Vanessa ignored the rest of what Emily had said and took off.

She found Courtney unlocking her car a couple of blocks away on a dark side street. Vanessa called out her name, and Courtney paused. Then she pulled her door open once the voice registered.

"Court, can you *please* just hear me out for five minutes?"

Courtney stopped and turned to face Vanessa. Her mouth was puckered, her jaw rigid. Fierce determination was etched into her expression, but she refused to make eye contact. She stared down at the keys in one hand while clutching a chunky shawl with her other hand, covering up her bare shoulders that Vanessa had been staring at in that black V-neck tank top all night.

"I'm doing the best I can here, okay?" Courtney said. "I'm not mad, but I'm being realistic. You're who you are, and I'm who I am. There's nothing else to talk about. Not if we want to keep the band intact." Her expression softened and a small smile appeared as she raised her gaze to look at Vanessa. "I'm trying really hard to be your friend. Because I want that. I do. But that's all I can do right now, and rehashing the same stuff over and over isn't going to help anything."

Vanessa couldn't think of a single thing to say in

response. She'd wanted to plead her case. To convince Courtney to forgive her. Or to at least stick around and have a drink as friends.

But this was the best she could hope for.

If Courtney was willing to get past this and be her friend, that was all Vanessa could ask of her.

The only thing left for Vanessa to do was give her space.

She nodded in silence and watched as Courtney drove off a few moments later. Then she went back inside the bar to gather her equipment.

"You're both stubborn as hell," Nicole said from behind her drum kit. "You know that, right?"

"Why am I stubborn?"

"Because you won't tell her the whole story!"

"She'll just get more angry."

"You're not giving her a chance to have the complete picture." Nicole collapsed a metal stand and folded the legs in one smooth motion. "Why keep it a secret? She already isn't talking to you."

"Because I don't want to deal with the reaction if I tell her." Vanessa sighed. "And I don't want her to feel guilty. I did it for her. The arrangement stands."

"I wish you'd let her know so she could see this side of you." Nicole put the stand on the floor and walked over to place her hand on Vanessa's shoulder. "You deserve for people to know you're also the person I see. The person I've known for as long as I can remember. The person who's always felt she had something to prove to everybody and makes a mess of things because she doesn't know she's already enough."

Vanessa blinked back tears and choked on a sob threatening to escape. Nicole did know her better than anyone. But she was wrong about this. Vanessa still had a lot to prove.

"Looks like you're the only one here who believes that."

Nicole squeezed Vanessa's shoulder and guided her in the opposite direction. "Come on, you sad sack. I'm buying this round."

29

COURTNEY

THE FIRST MARKET IN NOVEMBER WAS AN enormous success. Tons of people had come out to City Park that Saturday, and most mentioned they were kicking off their holiday shopping early this year. It was a perfect fall day, so people were in a good mood and happy to stroll among the oaks and meander through the tents all morning, picking up gifts.

Courtney's sales confirmed this was the case. As she packed up, she realized it had been so successful that she hadn't prepared enough for the next couple of months. She'd have to kick her production up next week since the Thanksgiving weekend market would run through all of her stock.

Not that she was complaining about the extra sales. It was just that she knew she'd lose next weekend to the music festival and inevitable day-after crash, so she'd need to make the most of the week ahead.

But for now, all she wanted to do was go home and relax. Saturday afternoons after a market were some of the few times she allowed herself time off. Her feet usually hurt, and she was over-peopled. Every other Saturday afternoon was blocked off as recovery time. And sometimes the Sunday after, if it was a particularly busy market day. No making more products or signing up for shows or filling online orders. She and Lucas would order pizza and watch whatever garbage he wanted. She could suffer through explosions as long as he was safe on the couch with her, and she could exhale in peace for a few hours.

"Let me help you with that."

Courtney looked up to see Nicole grabbing the other end of the table and helping her fold and secure the legs.

"What are you doing out here?"

Arts markets weren't Nicole's scene. Courtney had never seen Nicole with a single piece of jewelry on her, and if she had to guess, her apartment walls were probably free of any artwork as well. The only artsy thing she'd ever heard Nicole talk about was a set of drumstick wind chimes a friend had given her for her birthday several years ago.

"Oh, you know. In the area," Nicole said. "Figured I'd say hi."

"You're shit at lying."

Nicole frowned. "Fucking hate it."

"So tell me why you're really here."

"You know I love you and Vanessa both, right?"

Courtney's heart seized up. She'd been trying not to think about Vanessa all week. After Courtney had made her intentions clear last Friday night, Vanessa had kept her distance. She didn't try to pull her aside or talk at rehearsal Thursday. It still stung to see her, and Courtney wanted more than anything to fix this somehow. But she knew it was unfixable. She just needed to get over it.

Talking about Vanessa wouldn't help that.

"I don't like where this is going," Courtney said. "But, yeah. I know."

"You also know I don't want to interfere or be involved in y'all's business, but it seems Vanessa already dragged me into this, so now I gotta dig all of us out of it."

The part about not wanting to be involved was true. Unless Nicole could boss someone around and tell them what to do for their own good. But mostly, Nicole did stay out of everyone else's private affairs.

It was the last part that made no sense. Nicole hadn't even known they were together for that short time, so Courtney didn't know what she was talking about.

"Dig us out?" she asked. "How did Vanessa drag you into anything?"

"I'm gonna tell you something, but it's killing me to do this behind her back. Although the only reason she's not going to tell you herself is because she doesn't want to mess things up for you. And dang it, I didn't want to be involved in the first place and said this was a bad idea from the jump."

"Nicole, what the hell are you talking about?"

"Remember how you were surprised we were getting paid more for those gigs than what we used to get?"

"Yeah."

"Well, we aren't getting more." Nicole waited for a second while that information sank in. "Vanessa made me give a big chunk of her pay to you every gig."

Courtney could only stare at Nicole while she absorbed each of those words and tried to make sense of them. But it was useless. No amount of absorbing or mentally rearranging them made any sense.

"Why would she do that?"

Nicole looked shocked, like it was the most ridiculous question she'd ever heard. "Because she thought you needed it more than she did. And, I guess, because she felt bad about bailing and breaking up the band and for you losing three years of gig money on account of her choice."

Courtney shook her head. "That doesn't make any sense. By that logic, we all lost out on band money."

"Yeah, but we don't all have a brother we're responsible for." With a frown, Nicole asked, "Are you really that dense? Or just that stubborn?"

Courtney would admit she was both sometimes,

but right now, she was only confused. "I still don't get it."

"She gave *you* the money because she cares about *you*. Shit, she was probably falling for you long before she even realized it. And I'm guessing the same goes for you, too."

That, Courtney understood. The part about denying her own feelings for a long time and feeling a deep sense of responsibility to fix things for other people. She'd just never considered either of those might be things Vanessa also felt.

"I didn't ask for any help."

"No, but you needed it, and she wanted to give it. Knew damn well you wouldn't take it, too. So she asked me not to say anything." Nicole sighed. "I never should have agreed, but I did. And damn it, I'm tired of being in the middle of this and watching you make assumptions without all the information."

"I don't see how this changes things."

Nicole laughed. "Stubborn it is then."

"I'm serious. It doesn't change the fact that we didn't work out," Courtney said. "In fact, it's just another example of her doing what she wants and not being honest about it."

"Oh, drop it." Nicole abandoned any hint of a joking tone. "You were mad because you thought she was being selfish. Yes, she should have been honest about it. That's on her. But she wasn't being selfish. She took those gigs with Kings of Canal because she needed the money after putting you first."

"And impulse-buying a bird."

"Oh my gosh, you really are dense too." Nicole rolled her eyes. "She's wanted one of those damn birds for as long as I can remember. You know that. Now, I'm not a fan of the thing, but I'm glad she gave it a home. It was abandoned, and she was lonely and lost. She and that bird needed each other."

When Nicole put it like that, it kind of made sense. Courtney knew Vanessa had always loved those birds, but she'd never considered why she wanted to have Bob now, at this point in her life.

And if Vanessa hadn't been sending half her share to Courtney, she might not have needed to take those other gigs to help pay for his care.

"So you're saying she really didn't want to play with them again? She wasn't lying about that part?"

"Hell, no! She's miserable any time she's with them. Took her a while to admit it the first round, but she got there eventually. This second round with them was strictly business. Held her nose and suffered the stink for the cash."

Courtney had assumed Vanessa wanted to play with them again, and the money was just an excuse. Like when someone insists they don't want their ex or some other person, but half a second after a breakup, they're hooking up with them.

She put a hand on the remaining table she hadn't

folded up yet and steadied herself as the park and all the other vendors swirled around her like a carousel.

Except she wanted off of this ride.

Courtney was still struggling to make sense of everything. Not just what happened, but how she hadn't pieced it together. How she'd misjudged Vanessa.

She might not understand everything, but she knew what needed to happen next.

"First of all, cut that shit out and stop giving me her money."

"Uh-huh," Nicole agreed. "What's second?"

Second was a lot harder. Second meant facing her fear. She'd been so afraid Vanessa would leave again. So afraid that she would be left behind like her mother had done with her and Lucas, that she hadn't given Vanessa a chance. Not a real one.

"Second is I fix this."

Nicole smiled. "Good. Let me help you carry this shit to your car, so I can make sure you don't chicken out."

"I could still chicken out after you leave."

Nicole grabbed a tote filled with smaller plastic containers. "You won't. Once you make a decision, you'll follow through."

"So helping me carry this isn't just to make sure I don't chicken out?"

"Good grief, Court. It's because you won't accept

help from anyone unless we lie to you about it. Haven't you been paying attention?"

Courtney laughed and shook her head. "I'll try to work on that, too."

"Good." Nicole gave her a wink. "Y'all can work on your shit together."

30

VANESSA

A coworker stopped Vanessa as she was clocking out and grabbing a coffee to take home. One of the many perks of this job she'd grown to love. The complimentary coffee was to die for, and her coworkers were a laid-back mix of college students and older downtown hipster types. She'd been a little wary, but they'd proven to be a cool bunch.

"You got a gig tonight?"

Vanessa shook her head and took a sip from her to-go cup as she addressed the twenty-something in overalls, a blue and white striped shirt, and long turquoise pigtails. "Off this weekend. You're still good to cover my shift next Saturday, right?"

"The Artemis music festival thing. Yeah, definitely." The young woman nodded toward the other end of the counter where a barista was handing finished drinks to customers. "Want to come to a party tonight?

Me and Riley and a few other people. Nothing too wild."

Vanessa wondered if her definition of "nothing too wild" still matched up with her coworker's idea of what that meant. She felt like the old lady around here. And she was about to reinforce that image.

"Thanks, but I'm gonna have to pass this time. I'm pretty tired, and Bob and I have a hot date."

"Bob?"

Vanessa laughed. "My bird?"

"Oh, right. I forgot about that thing. I'd tell you to bring Bob along, but Riley's cat is a fucking menace."

"I appreciate the offer," said Vanessa. "Maybe next time?"

"Sure," she said. "You and Bob have a good night off!"

Vanessa planned to have a good afternoon and evening on her couch with that bird she'd already fallen head over heels for. He really was the sweetest thing now that he'd settled in with her. She let him out as often as she could whenever she was home, and he loved to perch on her arm while they watched TV together. And he liked classic rock almost as much as she did. He was the perfect roommate.

It wasn't the same as having a person to snuggle on the couch with. Especially now that the days were getting cooler and it would be nice to cozy up under a blanket with another warm body in the evenings. But life with Bob was still pretty great.

She maneuvered through the coffee shop crowd to step outside and absorb the sun's rays like a lizard. She loved the coffee shop, but the air conditioner blasted every afternoon, even in early November. A welcome respite for folks drinking hot drinks in a building that was built like a greenhouse, but her skin felt tight and dry and craved sunshine and moisturizer by the end of her shifts.

Vanessa's phone buzzed in her hand. When she looked down at it, her heart clenched and her stomach twisted in an anticipatory knot. The text message was from Courtney.

Are you home? Need to drop something off for you.

Her phone hadn't lit up with that name since they'd ended things after rehearsal last week. She hadn't heard a word from those lips after Courtney had told her there was nothing left to talk about.

But Vanessa had a lot left to say.

Still, she'd decided to give Courtney some space and wait for the right time. She didn't want karmic credit for the money situation, but she wanted to come clean about it. She wanted to be honest about everything with Courtney. Everything in the past and everything from here on out. Whether they were friends or romantic partners, she needed to be up front about it all. They both deserved honesty.

Maybe this was that right moment she'd been waiting for. She didn't know what Courtney might be dropping off, but it at least meant she was willing to see Vanessa. Maybe she'd also be willing to hear her out.

Vanessa would have to do this carefully. A short explanation. To the point. No rambling.

She texted back that she'd be there in ten minutes, then hustled to her car a couple blocks down the road, preparing her speech and perfecting the delivery of it along the way.

VANESSA PACED BACK AND FORTH, cutting a path through her living room carpet while practicing her speech out loud. This was her third full run through it, changing only a few words here and there.

She'd put Bob in his cage, so he wouldn't be startled by the door knock or fly around when she opened it. He whistled and clucked at appropriate pauses and gave his signature, "That's awesome," approval each time she finished and asked what he thought of her speech.

A knock on the door cut her off.

Courtney stood on Vanessa's doormat, holding a white envelope in one hand. She wore a chunky gray open-front sweater over a tight black T-shirt, and what Vanessa had previously learned was Courtney's favorite pair of light wash jeans. Her eyes held a strange mix of hesitance and intensity, and her blonde bob was freshly trimmed but untamed. A perfect mix of all things Courtney.

Despite all of her rehearsing, Vanessa found that she couldn't form words. She'd been practicing her speech, but she didn't plan what to say at *this* moment. Vanessa wasn't much of a planner anyway, so this whole preparation thing was shorting out her brain.

She just stepped aside and waved a hand to invite Courtney inside.

Relief washed over Vanessa as Courtney walked across the room to stare into Bob's cage, remembering to put her hands behind her back as she spoke softly to him.

"Hey, Bob. Missed you, little guy."

"That's awesome!"

Bob was delightful, but the bird had no grasp of context.

Courtney laughed and turned around to face Vanessa. It was clear she was equally lost for words.

Prepared words or not, Vanessa had to say something. This was her mess, and it was time to clean it up.

She had to push aside any fear that she might push Courtney even further away... maybe even for good. But Courtney deserved the truth. And she deserved someone who trusted her enough to be honest with her.

When Courtney raised her hand with the envelope, Vanessa held up her own hand and said, "Wait. I need to tell you something first."

Courtney paused a second, then nodded.

"I never lied to you," Vanessa said, taking a deep breath before barreling into the rest of her speech. "I didn't want to play with Kings of Canal again, but I did need the money. In part because of something I should have been more honest with you about." She bit the inside of her mouth, stalling and gathering the courage to continue. "I've realized that I want that. Honesty. I want honesty and openness in heart and mind and words and actions in a relationship, and I didn't fulfill my end of that with you. Not completely."

She gestured at the couch, and Courtney sat facing her from the opposite end.

Vanessa took another deep breath and continued. "I convinced Nicole to give you half of my gig money and not tell you where it came from. I swear, I meant well by it. I wasn't trying to manipulate you or buy you off. I really did just want to help you and Lucas out in some small way. The only way I could think of. But I should have thought harder. Or, at least, I should have told you about it once we were together. So, I'm sorry I wasn't completely honest with you about that." She exhaled what little air she had left in her lungs, feeling the weight of her confession leaving her body along with it. "And that's it. I swear. You know everything now. Everything else I've told you, everything I said I felt... it was all real. And now you know the whole truth."

There was a long stretch of silence that Bob eventually filled with more whistles and clicks. Courtney didn't acknowledge the noises. She held her gaze steady on Vanessa. She didn't appear angry, but Vanessa couldn't quite read whatever emotion was behind those intense eyes of hers.

"Thank you for telling me." Courtney gave a small appreciative smile, then added, "But I already knew that."

31

COURTNEY

She watched as Vanessa absorbed her words. Vanessa's dark eyes stared intently, studying Courtney's face. Courtney just sat across from her on the couch and let Vanessa peer inside her.

The whole drive over, she'd been worried about how she would say this. She'd rewritten a speech four different ways in her head, and nothing sounded right. Finally, she'd decided to let her heart speak.

When she'd arrived, it was Vanessa who did the talking for her.

Courtney had been so concerned that she'd waited too long to figure this out. Like Nicole said, she never had all the information. But Nicole was also right about Courtney being stubborn. Which was probably why Vanessa didn't want to tell her about the money or the gigs in the first place. Courtney didn't have the best track record for handling news well.

Vanessa finished processing and said, "You... already know?"

"That's what I came here for." Courtney held out the envelope she'd brought with her. "This is yours."

Vanessa took the envelope and peered at the cash inside. Courtney had gone straight to the ATM after she'd spoken with Nicole and pulled out enough money to repay Vanessa for her share of all their gigs so far. Courtney hadn't touched any of it since she'd taken the bonus as an opportunity to bulk up their emergency savings. But it was never hers to hold, and she was glad she had it to return to its rightful owner.

Vanessa shook her head. "This isn't why I told you about the money. I don't want it back."

"I know. I believe you. But it's still yours, and I can't keep it. You already know that, which is in part why you didn't tell me." Courtney took a breath to gather her courage and offer an apologetic smile as she said the rest of what she came here for. "The other part of why you didn't tell me is because I can be a terrifying, immovable jerk sometimes."

Vanessa laughed. "I would say fiercely protective of yourself and those you love. Your solid boundaries are what make you a good sister and friend."

"Not so much a good friend lately," Courtney admitted. "Those boundaries keep me safe, but the spikes keep everyone out. Even people I care about."

Vanessa made a sheepish shrug. "Well, some of us gave you good reason to install extra spikes."

Courtney had been right to question Vanessa after her return. She wouldn't apologize for that. But when she'd given Vanessa a chance, Courtney hadn't really been open to the possibility that she had changed. And Vanessa had already proven her loyalty to the band. Even if she chose to pick up a few gigs with her old band, she'd been telling the truth about not wanting to play with them anymore. Courtney just hadn't been listening.

"Maybe. But I wasn't really open. Wasn't *really* giving you a chance. Deep down I was waiting for— maybe even looking for—proof that you didn't care. That this was all temporary."

"I always cared." Vanessa scooted across the couch and took Courtney's hand. "And I know you won't believe it, but I never thought of you as temporary. Never."

"I need you to know that it wasn't just you." When Vanessa looked confused, Courtney added, "I think everyone is temporary. Or at least their intentions are temporary. I've gone through the last decade—more than that—believing that everyone leaves eventually."

Vanessa held her gaze, sadness and understanding apparent in her eyes. "You don't leave. You stick by the people you love. I watch you do it every day with Lucas. You'd never bail on him. And I'm trying to prove that I'm not leaving either. I'm not bailing on you."

"No. I'm the one who bailed on you. Because I was

convinced you would leave, so I beat you to it. And I was convinced us being together and breaking up might ruin the band."

"You were scared," Vanessa said. "Don't be so hard on yourself. Besides, we did get together and break up, and we didn't tank the band."

Courtney blinked back tears threatening to spill over. She hadn't considered how one of her biggest fears really *had* come true, and the consequences weren't the worst-case scenario. She should have trusted her bandmates could handle this. Just like she should have trusted Vanessa a little more.

"I don't want to live in that fear. I want to be happy. And to do that, I need to let go of the past— mine and yours—and let the present and future be what they are."

Vanessa gave a hesitant, curious grin. When she spoke, her voice was full of fearful hesitancy. "Does that present include me?"

"If you'll forgive me for being a stubborn, fearful jerk?"

"Only if you'll forgive me for being an impulsive, selfish scaredy-cat." Vanessa scooted close and took Courtney's face in her hands, looking her in the eye. "I don't know what the future holds, but I want to discover it all with you. If you're willing to take the chance and discover it all with me."

Courtney felt a swell of hope rise in her chest. It

had been so long since she'd allowed herself to indulge in hope.

She moved a hand against the couch to slide it around Vanessa's waist, then leaned in to kiss her. She poured her whole heart and all of her hope into that kiss. But she wasn't empty. Hope poured right back to her from Vanessa's lips.

"That's awesome!" Bob squawked from across the room.

Their kiss dissolved into rolling laughter.

Then Courtney touched her forehead to Vanessa's and said, "Deal."

32

VANESSA

Vanessa climbed another step and peered at the crowd gathered in Lafayette Square. She was happy to be on a big stage again, but she was even happier to be on *this* stage.

Artemis Live was everything they'd been promised. It had an amazing lineup of bands and vendors, all supporting a cause she believed in. A wide variety of pride flags hung from tents spread around the park to remind everyone that they were all there to support the queer youth of New Orleans.

"Don't hog the view," Libby said, clamoring over Vanessa's shoulder. Her high, poofy pigtails bumped against the side of Vanessa's face as she jostled for her own look at the crowd. "Jeez, that's a lot of people."

Their Friday night audience that crammed inside that tiny bar were nothing compared to this. Outdoor shows were always something special, and this festival was definitely a hit.

"No fair! I can't see," Emily whined from the bottom of the steps.

Nicole and Courtney waited on the ground near the stairs, Nicole shaking her head and smiling, while Courtney picked at the ends of her hair.

"Here, take my spot." Vanessa squeezed around Libby and Emily and descended the stairs. She took one of Courtney's hands and kissed it. "You have nothing to be nervous about."

Courtney snorted. "Says you."

"Yes, says me. And I know you pretty well, so I get to be a judge on this. I've heard you sing for the last two months, and you sound better than ever."

Vanessa had forgotten how nervous Courtney would get before a big event. Like everyone would find out she was a fraud or something equally ridiculous.

"You're also biased." Courtney smirked. "You kind of have to say nice things to me."

"Bullshit," Vanessa said with a grin. "It's also my job to let you know if you're showing your ass in public. Happy to know I'm the only one who'll be seeing that tonight."

Courtney laughed. "Promise?"

"Bet your ass." Vanessa gave her a quick kiss. "But seriously, you're going to be great. And I can't wait for everyone to hear the new song. You made some magic with that."

"What if they hate it?" Courtney tugged at her hair again. "What if they only like us when we play other people's songs? What if I'm just fooling myself writing this stuff?"

"Nonsense." She took the hand tugging at Courtney's hair and kissed it again. "But there's only one way for you to find out for sure."

Courtney bit her lip, unconvinced. "Seriously, what if they hate it?"

"But what if they love it?"

Courtney glanced toward the crowd and contemplated that. Vanessa had never met a crowd she didn't love. Never shied away from the cheers and applause. But Courtney needed a little more convincing that those things were waiting for her at the end of a performance.

Vanessa was happy to do that convincing. She'd gladly give this same pep talk or some variation before every show if that's what it took to get Courtney on that stage. The world deserved her voice, and Courtney deserve the praise. She deserved to have her dreams come true. In this case, her dream of singing her own words and having her song played for a crowd.

Vanessa had finally realized she had everything she wanted right in front of her. She didn't need to chase bigger stages or bigger audiences anymore. Only the right stage, with the right bandmates, playing for the right crowd. She didn't have to prove anything to anyone. Certainly not her family. She had all the family she needed right here with her. This was what she'd been missing. And the fact that she was getting to play alongside the woman she loved was sprinkles on the best rock music sundae ever.

Yeah, she loved Courtney. She just hadn't told her yet. But she planned to as soon as this show was behind them. She didn't want Courtney to question or doubt for even one second the words were sincere. If she said it too close to this event, Courtney might suspect Vanessa was caught up in the excitement of it all. But Vanessa had known she'd fallen for Courtney the moment she'd lost her. She just hadn't been ready to admit it then. And she didn't want to scare Courtney off when she'd shown up at her apartment last week, so she'd decided to take things one baby step at a time. At a Courtney pace. She could do that. Vanessa could wait as long as Courtney needed for every step along the way, as long as they took those steps together.

"Everyone ready to go?" Jo stood behind them, chugging a water bottle and grinning ear to ear. Her band was playing last, but she was offstage with each of the groups, hyping them all up for each of their performances. "The turnout is great, right?"

"Amazing," Courtney said. "Bryn did an outstanding job pulling all of this together."

"I think so, too." Jo nodded toward the stage. "She's about to announce y'all. Ready?"

Vanessa looked to Courtney, who paled but nodded at Jo. Vanessa gave her hand a squeeze and spoke for them both. "Hell, yeah. Let's do this."

EPILOGUE

Courtney vibrated with anticipation as Molly closed the door behind her, leaving Lucas inside a room full of cats.

Vanessa chewed her thumb beside her, equally impatient to hear what was happening on the other side of that door. Courtney had noticed she stopped chewing them over the last few weeks, but the habit reared its head again whenever she was nervous. It warmed Courtney's heart to know that Vanessa cared so much about Lucas, too.

Molly turned to face them with a big grin beaming from above her Westbank Animal Warriors T-shirt.

Courtney couldn't wait another second to hear how it was going in there. "Think he'll find the right one?"

With a firm nod, Molly said, "Got several sweet young adult cats in that room. They all went right up and introduced themselves. They're excited to see a new face, but they're all fairly independent. Not too needy or anything after their initial greetings. Pretty sure he'll find a match in there."

The relief in her shoulders surprised her. She hadn't realized how tense she'd become waiting outside the room while her brother met what might be his new cat.

He'd brought up that he wanted a pet just before last week's semester finals. They'd never had pets growing up, but it was more than curiosity for Lucas. He had already talked it over with his therapist before bringing it up to Courtney, and they'd all agreed the calming companionship and the responsibility of pet ownership could be good for him.

They'd discussed all kinds of animal options, and he was clear that he didn't want something that would live in a tank or a cage. He wanted a pet that might snuggle with him while he studied or watched videos, but also something that was lower maintenance than a dog. Since Courtney didn't want to get stuck walking a dog while he was at class or work, she agreed.

So Courtney had gotten Molly's number from Vanessa and set up a meet and greet at the shelter as soon as his finals were over. The adoption fees for this cat would be her early Christmas present to him.

Molly nodded to another door. "I'm gonna check on some other guys and be back out in a minute. He can stay as long as he wants in there."

She disappeared into the other room, then a second later, both Courtney's and Vanessa's phones dinged with a message.

Vanessa got to hers first. "Nicole. She sent the setup time for that private party this weekend."

Courtney was glad to concede that Vanessa had been right. The Artemis Live crowd had *loved* their performance. Nicole had been answering booking requests throughout the past few weeks from people who'd seen them at the festival or had heard about their show. Now their schedule was packed with holiday and upcoming Mardi Gras season bookings.

The steady flow of cash put Courtney in a much more comfortable financial position, and she'd built up a little more savings. She was still doing all the art markets and online orders. That was a creative outlet she'd probably never give up, no matter how successful the band became.

Not that she wanted huge amounts of fame, nor were they anywhere near the level that Jo's band was at. Still, Courtney had to admit, success at this level was pretty freaking sweet.

"While I'm here, I wanted to show you this." Vanessa tapped and scrolled until she found what she was looking for, then she held the phone screen against her chest. "I found something that I think is perfect, but it requires some explanation."

Courtney struggled to interpret what was behind Vanessa's excitement. "You're scaring me a little."

"Don't be scared. Just remember, this is not scary." She hesitated for a moment before handing the phone to Courtney. "Take a look at this."

The image on the screen was a real estate listing for a rental close to Courtney's place. Her heart fluttered with the idea of Vanessa so close by, but her brain spun with the logistics. It was much bigger than Vanessa's current apartment. "Can you really afford it?"

Even though the band was doing well, Vanessa had kept her job at the coffee shop. She'd insisted it was because she enjoyed the work and talking to customers and her coworkers every day.

Courtney didn't remember her mention wanting out of her apartment. She and Bob seemed pretty cozy there every time Courtney visited.

Vanessa's mouth stretched into a hesitant grin. "No. But *we* can."

"We?" The word came out as a gasp. Despite spending almost all of their free time with each other this past month, they hadn't talked about moving in together, much less moving to a *new* place. "You want to—"

"Yes!" Vanessa grabbed Courtney's free hand in both of her own. "I don't want to scare you, and I know you'll need time to consider this. But I have been thinking about this. This isn't a whim. And I think this place would be perfect."

Her enthusiasm was intoxicating, and Courtney wanted to drink it in and follow her wherever she was going. The more she allowed herself to sink into the comfort of this relationship, the more enamored Courtney became with Vanessa's ability to charge toward what she desired.

Courtney had seen it as a flaw before, but the more she explored how Vanessa worked, the more she realized that Vanessa wasn't ruled by thoughtless impulses. She was driven by passion and quicker processing. That didn't mean she couldn't give things thorough consideration. Only that she didn't spin on those thoughts, second-guessing from every angle like Courtney did. It's what made them a great team. Courtney could spot all the roadblocks up ahead, and Vanessa could keep them moving toward what they wanted once they calculated the risk together.

From the sound of it, Vanessa had done the calculations on her own before floating this idea, but Courtney needed a moment to do the same.

All she could do now was stare and blink at Vanessa. Not sleeping the night before wasn't helping on the processing front. Success and love hadn't magically cured her insomnia. But she'd seen a doctor to rule out physical causes, and she'd already started sessions with Lucas's therapist to see if maybe talking things out might help a little.

"But..." Courtney wasn't sure what the rest of that sentence was yet, but something was holding her back. Something that wasn't her feelings for Vanessa, because she was all in with that.

"It's okay. I know you need time to figure everything out. I just want you to see this place and how perfect it would be," Vanessa said. "If you're ready."

Was she ready?

Courtney was almost never ready. She just had to leap, anyway.

And that had worked out for her with the band reunion and with Vanessa. Maybe she didn't need to feel fully prepared for this, either.

"It looks nice," she said, staring down at the screen again. The entire building was larger than what Courtney had now, but the square footage and price weren't matching up. "Is it for half the duplex?"

Vanessa shook her head. "The whole thing. You and me and Bob could have one side, and Lucas and his cat could have the other side. Lucas would still be close by to eat all our food, but he could have some independence this way."

Courtney looked up at those expectant eyes again. Vanessa really had thought all this through before presenting it.

"Is there space for me to work outside?"

"Plenty," Vanessa said with a big grin. "You can scroll through the photos. They've got some nice pics of the backyard."

Courtney let herself get swept away with that grin. This place did look great. And as much as she loved the comfort of her current home—the only place Lucas had ever known—this would give them a chance to put some ghosts behind them.

She looked at the rent again. She loved Vanessa and trusted that she was all-in on this relationship, but Courtney had to consider the worst-case scenario.

If things didn't work out for whatever reason, this would be more rent than Courtney was paying now. But she was pretty sure she and Lucas could still swing it on their own. If they *had* to. And it was still a rental, so they could always find another place if necessary.

Courtney tried not to beat herself up for having to consider all that. She trusted Vanessa and wanted a future together, but her brain needed to work out all possible paths before it could jump on board with something like this.

The difference now was that while she was still making sure she had contingency plans, she wasn't *expecting* the worst to happen. She knew what her off ramps were, so she could drive past them, moving through her life filled with hope and a sense of security.

"I do need to think and talk to Lucas about it, but it looks great." Courtney handed back the phone and smiled at Vanessa. "Whatever we decide, I love you for this."

Vanessa tucked her phone into her pocket. "I'll send you the listing to look over this weekend and show Lucas. If you're both in, I want to pay the deposit myself."

"I couldn't let—"

"Yes, you could," Vanessa said firmly. "Think of it as my Christmas present to you both."

Something gnawed at Courtney's gut, but before she could grasp what it was, Vanessa read her expression and identified it first.

"If it helps your decision, I want your name alone to be on the lease," Vanessa said. "To be clear, I'm not going anywhere. I plan to stay with you as long as you'll have me by your side. I'm thinking... oh... forever?" She gave a playful grin before continuing. "But I want you to feel comfortable and know where all the emergency exits are. And I don't want you to feel stuck with me because of paperwork or logistics. I want to move in together and know that I'm there because you want me to be there. And I want you to feel that way, too."

Someone else might find that kind of practical decision-making unromantic or a warning sign, but those words were music to Courtney's ears.

"But what about you?" Courtney asked. "This looks perfect for me and Lucas, but are you sure this is what you want? That you won't get bored waking up to me every single day?"

They'd started talking more about Vanessa's tendency toward restlessness in a nonjudgmental way. It helped them both to acknowledge it and accept it as a vibrant part of Vanessa, just like everything else about her. It was the part of her that reminded Courtney to have fun and take a break from her responsibilities once in a while. And as long as they talked about it, it didn't scare Courtney anymore.

"Are you kidding me?" Vanessa said. "The mornings I get to wake up next to you are my favorite mornings. And every time we do something together, it's a new adventure for me to experience it with you. We've got new gigs and I see new customers at work every day and I get to come with you guys and watch Lucas get a cat! I haven't been bored for a single day in the last month. I can't imagine ever being bored in a life with you, but if that day comes, we can talk it out and hop in the car for a quick trip somewhere or host a backyard party or something else fun. There isn't a single thing we can't work out together."

Courtney's heart pounded and the blood rushing to her brain made her dizzy with excitement for their future. She closed the space between them and slipped her hands around Vanessa's waist. "Have I mentioned that I love you?"

Vanessa laughed and leaned in so her face was only inches from Courtney's. "Only every day."

With a shake of her head, Courtney said, "That's not nearly enough. I love you. And I plan to love you forever if you'll have me that long."

She kissed Vanessa, sending the full meaning of those words with that kiss, hoping the message got through.

Vanessa kissed her back, then pulled away and smiled, pure bliss on her face. "I love you forever, too."

<hr>

Join Leigh's monthly newsletter
to receive a FREE ebook collection, adorable foster cat photos, updates, and
sneak peeks of upcoming books:

http://leighlandryauthor.com/newsletter/

Rim Shot Rebound

Squeeze Box Belle

Complete Cajun Two-Step Box Set

ABOUT THE AUTHOR

Leigh Landry is a contemporary romance and mystery author who loves stories with happy endings, supportive friendships, and adorable pets. Once a musician, freelance writer, and English teacher, Leigh now spends her days writing and volunteering at an animal rescue center in the Heart of Cajun Country.